A Ticklish Affair

Praise for the book

With consummate skill, Sunil and Sudhir hold the attention of their readers as they spin romantic, mysterious and tragic tales that do not 'tax' the reader. An 'unputdownable' compilation of stories about human frailties, lives and loves is another colourful feather in the authors' shared cap.

—**Man Mohan, Roving Editor, *The Sunday Guardian***

What touches the heart is the simplicity with which the authors build the characters, making the whole plot so relatable! With their untypical writing style, Sunil Kapoor and Sudhir Kapoor truly democratize literature. This book is highly simple, sentimental and truthful.

—**Varun Khanna, Director, Bikman Constructions**

The stories are so real and in tune with human emotions, that it bellies the concept 'work of fiction'. The stories retain focus, move at a fast pace and have an intense impact. The twists, turns and the uncharacteristic romance are narrated by the twin craftsmen in their inimitable style.

—**Sujoy Mukherjee, Joy Mukherjee Productions**

The stories in this book invariably lead you to reminisce about events in one's own life. I was reminded of Blaise Pascal who wrote, 'The heart has its reasons, of which reason knows nothing.' The book also reminded me of Rumi, who wrote, 'Be a witness, not a judge. Focus on yourself, not others. Listen to your heart, not the crowd.' I wish more power to the pen.

—**Lt Gen. P.K. Singh**

Sunil and Sudhir have always surprised me with their stories communicated brilliantly, portraying different aspects of life. The stories are not only engrossing but depict the authors' storytelling skills. *A Ticklish Affair and Other Stories* is a nerve-wrenching and heart-warming, brilliantly written book.

—**B.M.N. Sehgal, Developer**

Storytelling is an art, which the authors have mastered. The writers have expressed with their hearts as if the incidents had unfolded before their eyes! Their stories have a balanced and beautiful blending of relationship, emotion and betrayal. Reading 'Rickshaw Faridabadi' will confirm this.

—**Bhupinder Singh, Former Chairman, State Trading Corporation**

Among all the remarkable stories, 'Spark of the Divine' has stolen my heart. Unfolding in the most unexpected ways, it gives the reader strength to hold on to their beliefs. It engrosses the reader so much so that he drowns in the story, never wanting to resurface. I believe, when someone feels this way while reading a story, it seems to have served its purpose.

—**Suresh Raheja, Singer and Developer**

The authors demonstrate quite an imaginative style of storytelling. It is a highly intriguing and unputdownable collection of stories. The twins have poured their hearts out in every story. Written in an eminently readable literary style, the book deserves a wide readership. Stories like 'Rickshaw Faridabadi' and 'Blackmail' are tailor-made for Bollywood movies.

—**Deepak Seth, Chairman, Pearl Group of Companies**

Sunil and Sudhir have this rare knack of weaving incidents, which they have heard or experienced in life, into stories that grip the reader's attention right from the start. With their characteristic imagination, a peculiar circumstance or twist is introduced into the narrative, which further revels the reader's mind.

—**Lt Gen. Gurinder Singh**

The short stories are not only full of romance, colour, emotions, but at the same time, exciting and sensuous. 'Rickshaw Faridabadi' has sweet overtones of love, while 'The Kikar Tree' unearths the unscrupulous methods adopted by some holy men. The authors have depicted the stories in such literary fashion that one can visually imagine the scenes.

—**Navin Ansal and Raseel Gujral Ansal, Interior Designers**

Short stories are a difficult genre to master and the authors have nailed it. The book is enjoyable to the core. The stories are engrossing and well worded. The authors deserve praise for their storytelling skills and imagination.

—**Ashwini Shanker, Amba Cinemas**

With this engrossing, well-written collection of short stories, Sunil and Sudhir have portrayed new thoughts and perspective in the readers' minds. The narrative is at times happy and at times sad, touching an emotional chord. The stories are intriguing, soaked in every colour of life.

—**Binoy Berry, Chairman, Contec Group**

A Ticklish Affair
AND OTHER STORIES

SUNIL KAPOOR & SUDHIR KAPOOR

RUPA

Published by
Rupa Publications India Pvt. Ltd 2019
7/16, Ansari Road, Daryaganj
New Delhi 110002

Sales centres:
Allahabad Bengaluru Chennai
Hyderabad Jaipur Kathmandu
Kolkata Mumbai

Copyright © Sunil Kapoor and Sudhir Kapoor 2019

Photo Courtesy: Authors' Collection

All rights reserved.

No part of this publication may be reproduced, transmitted,
or stored in a retrieval system, in any form or by any means,
electronic, mechanical, photocopying, recording or otherwise,
without the prior permission of the publisher.

This is a work of fiction. Names, characters, places and incidents are either the
product of the authors' imagination or are used fictitiously and any resemblance to
any actual person, living or dead, events or locales is entirely coincidental.

ISBN: 978-93-5333-681-3

First impression 2019

10 9 8 7 6 5 4 3 2 1

The moral right of the authors has been asserted

Printed at Parksons Graphics Pvt. Ltd, Mumbai

This book is sold subject to the condition that it shall not,
by way of trade or otherwise, be lent, resold, hired out, or otherwise
circulated, without the publisher's prior consent, in any form
of binding or cover other than that in which it is published.

Contents

Foreword	ix
Preface	xi
Blackmail	1
Let Me Soar High	32
Masqueraders from the North	51
Rickshaw Faridabadi	78
A Ticklish Affair	98
The Kikar Tree	118
Agnates and Cognates	135
Tiger Trail	154
Spark of the Divine	169
A Lover's Message	184
Acknowledgements	203

Foreword

It has been a pleasure to have read the writings of Sunil Kapoor and Sudhir Kapoor, and even more so, to have the opportunity to present a foreword for the same. It is a delight, not just because I have known the authors for so long, but because I believe deeply in the truth that they present.

I have known the twin brothers since my childhood, and it has pleasantly surprised me of their coming together to create something out of the box, without any qualms. Not just because of how foolproof all their ideas always tend to be, but also because how they are in person. They have never shied away from their creative sides and have proven, time and time again, just how talented they are. Having been successful in multiple fields—singing, filmmaking and writing—they have never let anything hold them back. I knew, after all, that their second book would be nothing short of brilliant.

Whether it is the story about karma as in 'Blackmail' or the triumph of good over evil as in 'Let Me Soar High', they leave one pondering over how things work in the real world, how sometimes the path to success, happiness and growth is hindered by obstacles. This book matters because of the harsh realities it has put forward and the way all of it has been presented. Neither do miracles take place nor do any coincidences make things all right again. Instead, it's the ambition, the hard work, the never-say-die attitude that can be seen in the protagonists of each story.

The effort of keeping the stories as close to reality as possible is inspiring. The writers have shown, through their work, how overthinking and being stuck at the same place can only do so much good. Like many of the protagonists in this book, one must realize that change is only possible once we dare to see past our failures, hardships and the wrongdoings. We are only as strong as our toughest battles.

I wish Sunil and Sudhir all the best and immense success with the launch of this book.

Rajan Kapoor
(Golden Peacock Group)

Preface

We live in a volatile world, to say the least—a world that believes in begetting money, irrespective of the means of obtaining it; a world that looks down on poverty-stricken people and upraises the rich and influential; a world that is run by ruthless politicians who believe in sacrificing the lives of the common people for the sake of their country. People do not realize that they cannot 'login' to reality or value little things such as having a cup of coffee with their family in the world of Internet. Big and heavy doors swing easily on small hinges and similarly, all long-term relationships remain alive and steady on small gestures of care and concern.

The authors of this book have had all along laid emphasis on social behaviour, morals and care for family, which, unfortunately, have lost their bearing in our society today. We sincerely feel that this world benefits people who have no egos, are ever forgiving, love truly and laugh whole-heartedly. From our first book, *The Terrible Twins* to *The Peacock Feather and Other Stories*, *Punam Ka Chaand* and now *A Ticklish Affair and Other Stories*, we have believed in the ideology of walking away from arguments, anger, failures and fear that stifle our dreams and poison our souls. All the stories in both books dwell on people's behavioural patterns. We firmly believe that embraces can easily dry tears, candles can rid us from the darkness, memories can last for years, and it is these little things in life that bring abundant happiness.

We were glad to have received phone calls from various producers and personalities of the Mumbai Film Industry, who are eager to turn these stories into films. This encouraged us to publish *A Ticklish Affair and Other Stories*, depicting various facets of life. Good stories can indeed inspire hope, ignite imagination and instil a love for learning.

The ten stories in this book are on the similar lines as in the first volume and convey the message that if someone wants to, they can carve their own happiness on a stone.

We are extremely delighted that Joy Mukherjee Productions, Mumbai, have bought the rights to 'The Gutka King' to make it into a web series and 'The Lover's Message' is also to be made into a feature film. One of the stories in this book, 'The Kikar Tree', has been written on the basis of a film to be produced by Immaculate Ideal Human Foundation. Yet, another story where one of the co-authors have acted and sung songs besides providing lyrics is 'Tiger Trail', produced by SR Series. This film stars Dharmendra and Rati Agnihotri, and is nearing completion. A short film made by Joy Mukherjee Production *Let Me Soar High* (*Ab Mujhe Udna Hai*) is based on a short story in this book. It has bagged twenty-three awards, including the prestigious Dadasaheb Phalke Award, Mumbai. At the Jodhpur Film Festival, for the same film, the authors have bagged the prize for the 'Best Story and Best Screenplay'.

We would like to dedicate this book to our parents Mr Shanker Kapoor and Mrs Rajni Kapoor, who have always tried to inculcate in us the good things in life.

Sunil Kapoor and Sudhir Kapoor

Blackmail

This intriguing whodunnit story portrays smart people who become rich and have the best of both worlds and those who are blackmailed and remain ordinary, leading sullen lives. The plot is full of surprises, is scintillating, intricate and has ever-twisting tales of a beleaguered husband and his over-ambitious wife.

This story has been taken up by a renowned film producer to be made into a movie. The producer has approached famous music directors Amjad-Nadeem, Mumbai, for creating the background score for the film, which would be out in 2019.

Senior Advocate Mudgil picked up a bundle of files from his table and threw them on the floor. The expression on his face clearly showed his exasperation, impatience and hurry to get on with his next case. 'I am not interested in representing your case in court anymore,' he yelled at his client. 'Your case was weak and now, you have lost it. If you don't vacate the house within thirty days, you'll have to face dire consequences.'

Raj Nath pleaded with folded hands, 'Sir, where will we go? We have been living in that house for the past thirty-one years! Where will I take my family? I cannot afford another accommodation.' He stood holding the shoulders of his fourteen-year-old son, Ravi, who had accompanied him to the lawyer's office, shaken and driven to tears.

Mudgil snapped, 'Haven't you enjoyed the benefits of staying there for so many years, on a paltry rent of sixty-five rupees? You've lived in that house since you came from Rawalpindi after the partition of India. How many more years do you wish to continue like this? These days, that house could easily fetch a monthly rent of over twenty thousand rupees.'

He continued to shout, 'I had told you that the best that I could do was to get an extension for another month. I cannot help you beyond that. You will have to move out. Enough is enough!'

'But as I understand, the landlord cannot evict us as per the Rent Control Act,' Raj Nath tried to convince his lawyer.

'Are you going to teach me the law? The landlord has filed a case against you under Section 14 of the Indian Penal Code, stating commercial use of the residential premises. Can you afford to file an appeal against the eviction order and pay a huge amount as court fee? You can't afford another lawyer like me, nor do you have the financial strength to fight this case in a higher court. Just don't waste my time. Take your files and engage a junior lawyer. I cannot help you anymore.'

Raj Nath didn't know how to react. He realized that his lawyer had betrayed him. Yet, he attempted to convince Mudgil. 'Sir, why did you submit a rejoinder saying that your client would vacate the house? You are aware that I am facing a financial crunch, and yet, you have brought me to this. You didn't even inform me before making that decision!'

Mudgil retorted, 'Is it my fault that you've become penniless and can't pay my fees? I'm telling you for the last time, pick up your files and leave. Go to someone else. Your relationship with me ends here. Is that clear to you, Raj?'

Raj Nath was suffering from Parkinson's disease—an illness that progressed with time. When under stress, his symptoms immediately intensified. Ravi looked at his father whose hands were trembling. He could not take this insult anymore. Earlier, the lawyer would respectfully address his father as Raj Saheb.

'Father!' burst out Ravi. 'Why don't you tell him that you saw our landlord, Madan uncle, here the other day? Ask him what he was doing here. Is Mr Mudgil representing us or Madan uncle? Ask him!' Ravi pulled at his father's arm.

The advocate burst out in a rage. 'How dare he! Raj, take your ten-year-old son out of my office at once! How dare he accuse me?! Is he indirectly trying to say that I have taken money from your landlord and have deliberately lost the case? How dare he cast aspersions on a senior advocate? I'm a man of integrity, and I'm telling you the harsh truth. You have lost!'

Ravi was not easily brushed away. He stood his ground. 'Sir, there is something called ethics, and I am not ten but fourteen years old. I am old enough to understand that you have betrayed my father. The way you speak to him says volumes about your integrity. You seem to be on Madan uncle's side, not ours. Your father was a sincere man. He never ever changed sides when it came to being loyal.'

Mudgil was beside himself with anger. 'Oh! So, now you are going to teach me ethics and the code of conduct? Why don't you file a complaint against me in the Bar Association? And, why don't you get my licence to practise cancelled? Are *you* going to teach *me*? You? Get out before I have both of you thrown out. Don't compare me with my late father. The way he practised law doesn't exist anymore.'

Raj Nath signalled his son to remain quiet. 'Sir, I am sorry that he has been disrespectful towards you. Please…please help us withdraw the rejoinder before the judge. We have no place to go but the streets.'

But Mudgil was not listening. He walked to his table, took out some papers from a drawer, sat down and began to read. Ravi picked up the files from the floor. He held his father's trembling hand and led him to the door. But, before stepping out, he turned to say, 'Mr Mudgil, we are leaving, but one day you will repent this.' And then, the two walked out of Mudgil's sprawling bungalow.

The house where Raj Nath lived could not compare with what his family had left behind in Rawalpindi, Pakistan. Back then, they were wealthy landlords. They had to leave behind all their money, jewellery and valuables. Now, they lived in a simple two-bedroom dwelling in Lajpat Nagar—a refugee colony in South Delhi—since they arrived in Delhi, in 1947. For years, the family endured difficult times trying to make ends meet. Finally, Raj Nath found good work and had begun faring reasonably well when he lost his job after a road accident that left him incapacitated. It was back to facing hardships, and now, he could not pay his lawyer's fees. But the family decided to not vacate the house, come what may.

A month later, as Mudgil had foretold, some policemen, court officials and a local commissioner, appointed by the court, landed at their door to evict them. The events that unfolded that day were humiliating and remained embedded in Ravi's mind for a long time. The landlord, supported by the police, barged into the house and began dragging out the furniture. They threw out household items—utensils, mattresses and clothes—on the road. Ravi, his parents Raj Nath and Sheila, and older brother Mohan were physically held and pushed out of their house. It had begun to rain; despite that, the neighbours came out to witness the drama—four people stood on the road outside their house, with their belongings strewn around them.

No one heeded Raj Nath's pleadings. Not only had he lost the case, he had also been booked for contempt of court for not vacating the house. This meant that if he did not pay the fine, he would have to serve a sentence of three months in jail.

The situation became too much for Raj Nath to bear. He suffered a massive stroke and fell unconscious. The neighbours came to the rescue and rushed him to the hospital. Some of them even pooled money for a spine operation that the doctors said was required immediately.

Raj Nath remained in the hospital for a few weeks. In the meantime, his wife and young sons were left to take charge of their lives. After the incident, they had taken shelter at Sheila's brother's house. Mohan was only sixteen, but being the older of the two boys, he felt that it was his responsibility to fend for his family. He dropped out of school and began working for a close friend of Raj Nath's, Bansal Saheb, at his office in Nehru Place. Bansal was a share broker, doing well in his business. Seeing the determination in Mohan's attitude, he started off at a monthly salary of ₹1,200. Mohan could now think of getting accommodation for the family. He took an advance against his salary and paid the security amount for a flat-on-rent close to his office in Kalkaji. His family shifted there. Ravi continued his school and studies. Everything seemed to be settling down. Sheila paid regular visits to her husband, who was still recovering at the hospital.

Forty days passed since the incident. Raj Nath was showing signs of improvement, but he was worried about how his family would pay the hospital bill. Sheila tried to reassure her husband that things were going well; that Mohan had begun earning, and they were now able to manage their daily expenses. 'Our sons will work hard and take us out of troubled waters. Everything will be fine. Please don't be depressed. You are getting better. You'll be home soon. Things are finally settling down and…,' Sheila suddenly stopped as she noticed that her husband was just staring at her. Raj Nath had gone still. He had stopped breathing. She shouted for the nurse who came running, and immediately summoned the doctor. Raj Nath was wheeled into the operation theatre and administered life-saving drugs. But he could not be saved.

Years passed by. Mohan learned the tricks of the trade by becoming Bansal's right-hand man. He was sharp with a sound knowledge of the leading Indian companies in the markets. His clients made good money on the speculation tips he gave them and trusted his advice. After fifteen years of hard work, Mohan decided to marry and start his own family.

By this time, Ravi had completed his studies supported by his elder brother. He worked as a sales executive at Union Lamps—a light-fixture manufacturing company. As part of his job, he travelled across the country to find buyers for his products. Following his brother's footsteps, he worked hard and gradually made his presence felt in the marketing circles.

Soon, Ravi was promoted as the Senior Sales Executive. He was a confident young man with an outgoing personality. He was honest and met his targets before the others. Thus, he grew in the hierarchy to become the regional sales manager within months of his first promotion.

The demand for their products hit an all-time high when Ravi's managing director collaborated with an American company. However, after some time, he began indulging in malpractices. The American partner supplied mercury—an integral component for making lamps. The managing director of Union Lamps would sell this mercury in the black market and pocket the money.

Ravi was not happy. The demand for their products in the market reduced drastically because poor quality lamps were being produced with substandard materials. He was against the illegal sale of light-fixtures, which was instructed by the managing director. Truckloads of light fixtures were removed from the factory at night and sold without invoices, so that they could pocket the profits and avoid paying taxes. Other instances of illegal profiting included the sale of 60-watt light bulbs marked as 90-watt bulbs to get a higher price in the market.

Ravi was a righteous man. He believed in delivering quality products to his customers, many of whom were loyal to their brand. He told his supervisors about the fall in sales, the sliding goodwill and the degrading image of the company in an attempt to save them. But they did not listen. Ravi resigned. Luckily, he joined another firm—one that was run with absolute honesty—immediately after where he fit in perfectly.

Both the brothers were doing well for themselves. The days spent as refugees, counting pennies and wondering how to survive, were in the past. Now, they owned apartments in Greater Kailash, South Delhi, and had enough money to afford a few luxuries. They were respected in society.

Sheila was ailing with a heart disease. She desperately wanted her younger son, who was thirty-two, to get married and settle down during her lifetime. Mohan had a son, and Sheila was delighted to have seen her 'grandson's face' before she died. The only desire she had left was to see Ravi start his own family. He was successful at work, drawing a handsome salary. There were no reasons for him to wait any longer, she thought. On a relative's suggestion, she asked Mohan to put in an advertisement in the matrimony column of their daily newspaper.

Among the many proposals Ravi received, he could not ignore one from Anamika Awasthy. She was so beautiful that he could not take his eyes off her photograph. She was extraordinary. She had porcelain skin with sharp features and almond-shaped eyes. She had long black hair. It was love at first sight! Ravi could not believe his luck. He had a good job, financial stability, happiness all around, and now, a proposal from a girl who could easily pass off as a movie star. He wondered why she took a liking to him. His picture in the advertisement was ordinary.

Ravi was blown over when they met at a restaurant in Connaught Place. Anamika stood tall and confident as a twenty-seven year old, wearing a pastel-coloured saree, carrying herself elegantly. She spoke more than he did. She worked at a multinational company and drew a high remuneration. She seemed a perfect combination of beauty and brains. Ravi could barely speak and fumbled most of the time. He considered himself as an ace salesman, one who could talk himself through any sales call, and yet, he had to make an effort to converse with her. He kept staring at the gorgeous woman sitting across the table, praying that she would agree to the alliance in spite of the fact that he was no match for her.

Ravi met her again in Connaught Place. This time he was more comfortable. They talked for a long time on various topics—from politics to films. As the conversation progressed over lunch, Ravi realized they had begun discussing the number of relatives they were going to invite to the wedding ceremony. Anamika told him excitedly, that she was planning to wear a deep pink and gold lehenga. He imagined how beautiful she would look.

Ravi's family was elated. Sheila began the wedding planning immediately. His friends were happy for him. They considered him lucky to have gotten such a good-looking woman. Ravi was ecstatic. Life changed for him. He was overwhelmed by his good fortune. He could hardly wait for the wedding.

Finally, the day arrived. The wedding was solemnized amidst a lavish ceremony in the presence of a large gathering. The wedding party ended way past midnight, after which the groom returned home with his bride, along with the rest of his family. As is tradition, the relatives gathered around the couple and played games the rest of the night.

After tea, Ravi and Anamika took the early morning train to Kalka, a small town, from where they journeyed in a railcar to Shimla. Ravi had booked a special room for their honeymoon at an expensive hotel. He was looking forward to spending time with his wife; just the two of them.

They arrived at their destination in the evening and checked into their room. Ravi took a shower before ordering an early dinner to their room. After the meal, he ordered a bottle of wine and poured it out for both of them. He moved closer to his radiant bride, but she held his arm, asking politely if they could talk a little before celebrating the occasion. Ravi happily agreed. He wanted to make her comfortable, rather than rush things. He had all the time in the world.

They talked for a long time. Almost two hours had passed before Ravi looked at the time. It was ten o'clock. He found it difficult to control his feelings, and, this time, as he reached out for his beautiful wife, there was a knock on the door.

'Now, who could that be?' Ravi did not like being interrupted. He opened the door. Rajiv Ranjan, Anamika's boss, stood at the door. Ravi was surprised to see him. Rajiv was forty-two years of age, taller and more handsome than Ravi. He had completed his engineering from IIT, Delhi, and held an MBA degree from Boston, USA. Ravi recalled that Rajiv had given them a huge amount as their wedding present just yesterday. He wondered why he was here.

'I hope I'm not late?' Rajiv walked into the room and looked at Anamika enquiringly. She ran into his embrace.

Ravi was shocked at his wife. Wearing her bridal bangles and her *mangalsutra*, his newly-wed bride was in the arms of another man.

'Not at all,' Anamika said to Rajiv. 'That's not possible as long as I'm alive, darling. I am and shall forever be yours.'

'Fine, then,' Rajiv said, turning to Ravi. 'It's time that you know that Ana...sorry, Anamika, is like my wife. She is two-months pregnant with my child. I don't like beating around the bush, so I'll make it clear to you. We are in love with each other,' he declared.

'What!' Ravi almost shouted. He was shocked. 'What is all this? What are you talking about? What kind of a joke is this?'

'I'm serious,' said Rajiv. 'Do you think I've come to your room on the first night after your wedding to joke around?'

Ravi was utterly confused. This was beyond his comprehension. 'But...I don't understand. Aren't you married? You have children!' Ravi was now fumbling for words. 'You, you...you can't just barge into my room and claim my wife to be yours. And Anamika...' Ravi now looked at his wife, 'Pregnant! What is he saying?'

Anamika looked at him and said, 'You'd better believe it. Every word that he said is true. I am pregnant with Rajiv's child.'

'But then, why did you marry me?!' Ravi shouted. 'What was the need for all this...drama?'

Rajiv walked up to Ravi and said, 'Yes, I'm married, but I'm going to divorce my wife, to marry Anamika. Till then, we have planned that she will stay with you, pretending to be your wife. Once my divorce is through, the two of you will get a divorce, and finally, she and I will get married.'

Ravi's head began to reel. It was too much for him to take. He sat down, head in his hands, still wondering how to react.

Rajiv continued, 'I would've divorced my wife earlier, but there are joint properties in our names. Not to mention the fact that she has a rich and influential father. Anyway, Anamika is pregnant with my child, and this is the best solution for us. So, she will stay with you and give birth to my child. When the time comes, she will be mine. I'm willing to pay any price for this. Name it and it will be yours.'

Ravi still could not understand what happened suddenly to his more-than-perfect life. Rajiv had just dropped a bomb without any warning.

He put his hand on Anamika's arm and tried to reason with her, 'Anamika, my dear, do you realize what he is doing to you? Don't you understand? He's probably using you to wriggle out of his own marriage. This is ridiculous! How can anyone do this?'

Anamika laughed. 'No, dear husband, it is exactly as Rajiv said. You are the one being used,' she said, removing his hand.

Ravi was now pleading with Anamika. 'How can you do this to me? You can't leave me like this. What will people say? And you're believing him? He's a womanizer. He will leave you just like he's divorcing his wife. Anamika, please understand, he is making lame excuses. If he wanted to marry you, he would have separated from his wife already.'

Ravi held her arm and tried to pull her away from Rajiv. But Anamika shook him off. 'Stop it, Ravi! Not a word against

Rajiv. I won't tolerate it. It's my first night after my wedding, and I am going to celebrate it with Rajiv in his room. I'm sorry, Ravi, but that's the truth. We've been in a relationship for the past three years, and we love each other. I'm only waiting for his divorce. We had planned all this. Till now, we've been successful. The rest will follow as planned. You have to act as we tell you to. You'll soon be free.'

Ravi started yelling, 'But I still don't understand. Why me? Why? Why in the world would I agree to whatever you're proposing? Oh, God! I've been so stupid! No wonder a beautiful girl like you agreed to marry me! It was him all this time,' said Ravi, pointing to Rajiv. 'You made me a scapegoat! I fell in love with you the moment I saw you. Everything you've said about our relationship, our wedding, our first night…has been a lie. I'll never forgive you! Your parents are such nice people. I can't believe you're their daughter!'

It was Anamika's turn to raise her voice. 'My parents!' She shouted bitterly. 'What do you know about my father? When my mother was away teaching at school, he was busy having an affair with his colleague. He has a daughter with her. Yes, I have a stepsister, Shweta, who is ten years younger to me. It took a long time for my mother to accept the truth. My father gave his colleague money so that she would go back to her hometown, but Shweta lives in our house. After my brother died, my father diverted all his attention to her. He doesn't even remember that he has another daughter—me!'

Ravi exclaimed, 'How did I get entangled with such a family? The father…now the daughter! Wow! What a family!' He laughed sarcastically. He sat down with his head in his hands, again. Suddenly, he realized, 'So, that's why you didn't touch the wine. You're pregnant!' And then he wailed, 'Anamika, you have cheated on me! You have ruined my life. I won't let you get away with this. I'm going to file a case against you and prove that you were expecting another man's child when you married me. I'm going to expose you…both of you…and put you in jail.'

Rajiv picked up the glass of wine meant for Anamika and took a sip. 'Hmm, this is fantastic!'

Then, he addressed Ravi, 'Look, Ravi, be practical. You and Anamika can live together under the same roof as friends. I'll provide you with a luxurious fully-furnished apartment with all the amenities you want. You can have a luxurious car, too. Your mother is a heart patient. She won't survive if she came to know that Anamika is carrying my child. So, you see, it's a win-win situation for all of us. I can even give you financial aid, in case you want to start your own business.'

'You skunk!' Ravi was furious and could not control himself. 'Gone are the days when I would have fallen for the apartment or money. My family is self-reliant. We have enough. You can't bribe me. I disown her,' Ravi said, pointing to Anamika. 'She is not my wife from this second onwards. She can leave this room and go anywhere she pleases. Both of you, get out of here and leave me alone! I've had enough, and I have made up my mind. Nothing is going to make me change it.'

'Not even the police?' Anamika had a smirk on her face. 'Or a sentence of ten years behind bars… Will that not change your mind?'

'What? What do you mean by "the police" and "behind bars"?' Ravi was puzzled. He did not like the way Anamika stood there smiling at him. Her eyes bore a cold look. 'What are you talking about?'

Anamika looked straight at him. 'Do you remember the accident that took place five years ago? At the Kalkaji-Nehru

Place crossing? It was a hit-and-run case. Weren't you the one driving a Maruti van that hit two people on a motorbike?'

Caught by surprise, Ravi blurted out, 'How do you know about the accident? How did you know I was driving the van?' He was clearly taken aback.

'I know because I was the pillion rider. And my brother, Prashant, was driving the bike. He was killed in that accident. I was injured, but I survived,' Anamika said.

'That wasn't me in the van....' Ravi tried to refuse.

'Oh, yes, you were!' Anamika interjected with conviction. 'I saw your face as clear as the day when you looked out of the window at the two of us lying on the road. I have remembered your face since then. Do you know you can be sentenced to ten years in prison for the crime you have committed? The police were unable to trace the van and its driver, so the file was closed as an unsolved hit-and-run case. We were taken to the hospital. My brother was declared dead. Haven't you seen his photograph on the wall in our sitting room? He was a victim of your rash driving. You killed my brother. His death shattered me. He was the only person who was close to me.'

'It was an accident. I had no intention of killing anyone...,' began Ravi, but Anamika interrupted him.

'Why else do you think I proposed? We were looking for a pawn for our plan. I saw your photograph and recognized you. I told Rajiv about it and both of us planned everything. Now you understand why you were selected, my dear husband? So, now you will do exactly what we tell you. You are not going to budge from here or even think of divorcing me. We are going to go through with our plan, and if you do anything stupid, you will face the consequences,' Anamika asserted.

Ravi had no choice but to accept that he was the culprit.

But he tried to wriggle out of the situation. 'Well, that accident did take place just as you said,' he said, 'and I was driving that Maruti van that hit your bike, but where is the proof? I will deny everything before the police. You can't blackmail me into accepting your preposterous offer based on that accident. You can't prove anything.'

'Oh, yes, we can!' Rajiv stepped forward. 'I've recorded everything that you've just said,' he added, holding up the recorder for Ravi to see. 'Are you going to deny this? You are in a hopeless position, Ravi. Just give in and listen to us, or spend the next ten years in jail. The choice is yours.'

Anamika let out a shrill laugh of triumph, 'It serves you right for what you did!'

Ravi looked at the two of them in despair. He was clearly beaten. He sat down quietly, wondering about the mess he had gotten himself into.

'It's okay, buddy,' Rajiv spoke, 'you don't have to feel so bad. Things happen. Look at Anamika. Her father is giving all his property and possessions to Shweta. Anamika will get nothing from him. But she will get a lot from me. I will take care of her.'

'I don't think so,' said Ravi. 'One day, you will abandon her just like you are leaving your wife now. Selfish people like you and Anamika eventually lead lonely lives. Mark my words,' he declared.

'Oh, we shall see! I have no regrets about my wife. We never got along. But I love Anamika and I will do anything for her. So, it is settled then…,' Rajiv continued with a tone of finality, pleased that their plan had worked so far. 'You will continue staying here in Shimla as planned, while she and I are together.'

Anamika smiled. 'Well, Ravi dear, it's very late. Go to sleep.

I'll be with Rajiv in his room and all the time during *our* honeymoon,' she said, having a good laugh.

'Anamika, one day you will repent for what you have done tonight,' said Ravi.

'Oh, no! You better consider this as your penance for killing her brother and getting away with it, so far at least. Remember that this recording is with me. You have been naïve and foolish falling into our trap, but if you try anything smart, you know the end result.'

Rajiv picked up Anamika's bag, and they walked out, leaving Ravi filled with remorse. He wondered how he was going to face his family, especially his mother.

Ravi did not see Rajiv or Anamika for the next four days. Then, Rajiv left for Mumbai, and the married couple returned to Delhi, pretending that all was well between them.

In a few days' time, Ravi and Anamika moved to the plush apartment in Gurugram provided by her company. Months passed. Anamika gave birth to Rajiv's child. Ravi became the father of a pretty girl who was named Sonia by her mother. Ravi immersed himself in work to forget about his unconsummated married life. But the one thing that he could not resist was the love that he felt for his little princess. He showered her with his affection. She was completely oblivious to everything that had happened, especially to the fact that Ravi, her doting father, was not her real father. Ravi met his mother and brother often but avoided any talk about his wife.

Ravi ignored Rajiv's periodic visits to the residence. He avoided thinking about his wife when she went to Europe or other destinations to attend to official work with her boss. Sonia began her schooling, and the little toddler was close to Ravi than to her own mother. By now, Anamika had risen in the hierarchy of her company and had travelled to almost all the major countries in Europe, where the company offices were situated. She had everything that anyone could ask for; a relationship, a life filled with travel, a fat salary and money for the asking.

∽

Five years passed by.

One day, Ravi met one of Anamika's colleagues who told him about the incident that happened between Anamika and Rajiv just a few days ago. She had slapped Rajiv, who is currently the director of the company, in front of some staff. What had transpired remained unknown but Rajiv, red-faced and embarrassed, left the office in a huff. There were rumours about Anamika falling out-of-grace with the high-profile director. Ravi was not surprised. He had always anticipated trouble between his wife and her boss.

That night Ravi found Anamika quite disturbed. She came into his room, holding her pillow.

'Can I be with you?' She looked at him, hopefully.

'Sure, it's your house. If you feel like discussing what happened in your office, you are welcome. But you are definitely not going to sleep here. You may leave the pillow in your room,' Ravi kept his voice steady.

'So, you've heard? It wasn't my fault. You won't understand, but he has neither divorced his wife nor does he seem to have an intention of marrying me. He has started avoiding me. Whenever I try talking to him, he pretends to be busy. He deserved to be slapped, that slimy creature. I heard that he's begun giving gifts to his new secretary, Julian.'

'This is exactly what I had told you on our first night. He

would never leave his wife. He has the best of both worlds. You were a toy in his hands—a toy willing to be exploited for money. The toy has been replaced by another better and younger version, that's all.'

'But now, I realize my mistake. I'm sorry for all that has happened. Please forgive me. I promise I will never see his face again,' Anamika begged, 'I will resign from the company immediately. I can't stand the sight of him anymore.'

'No, no, no! You are mistaken, Anamika. You could have had me, but you, of course, were carrying out a plan with your boss. You had made your choice before we got married. You have no place in my room or my heart. You insulted me on our first night, remember? So, how can you now even think of being with me? I will never forgive you. I love Sonia, I love my mother, my brother and his family, but I have no feelings for you. Selfish people like you lead lonely lives. Just leave. You have created so much turmoil in my life, and now you want me to take you back? You can go ahead and tell the police about that accident. No more blackmailing from you. I don't care anymore.'

Anamika couldn't change his mind. She tried but in vain. She had to accept the rejection from Ravi. She left his room in tears and could not sleep that night. Ravi, on the other hand, had one of the most restful sleeps he had had in a long time. Before falling asleep, he muttered out loud, 'You asked for it!'

The next day, Anamika did not leave her room. She drowned herself in tears and alcohol. She refused to eat anything or talk to anyone. In the days that followed, she was asked to leave the company as well as her accommodation. Ravi packed his belongings, took Sonia with him, and left to live in a flat he had taken on rent. Anamika, amidst her depressed state, managed to leave for Dubai where she had an apartment in her name—a courtesy of Rajiv. She wanted to get away from Delhi; away from the gossip in her circle of friends and ex-colleagues. She knew they had an idea of what had happened; that she was having an affair with her boss in spite of him being married, and how it had turned sour. Stories about her were doing the rounds. She could not face it anymore. Once in Dubai, she hoped to think things over about how she would take her life forward.

⌘

Early one morning, a black SUV had been waiting near a lonely stretch in Gurugram—the same road that Rajiv Ranjan took for his regular jogs to the neighbourhood park. He was walking back to his apartment when the SUV began to move towards its target. The driver pressed on the accelerator, and the vehicle turned left from the road onto the pavement, racing towards Rajiv. It hit him head on. Rajiv took a somersault and landed with a thud on the pavement, bleeding profusely. The impact broke his spine; he lay there, gasping for breath. The driver, seeing him move, reversed the car. This time, the SUV drove over him. Then, it sped away towards Delhi. There were only a few people on that road. They gathered around the lifeless body. It was a ghastly sight. The mangled body laid sprawled out, blood spilled everywhere. The police were called to take care of the situation and begin the investigations.

Inspector Ranbir Singh, a no-nonsense and honest police officer at the crime branch, was made in charge of the Ranjan murder case. He had a reputation for solving complicated murder cases, and he immediately dived into work.

Ranbir Singh rang the doorbell. Ravi opened the door to his two-bedroom house. The inspector requested his time so that he could ask some questions regarding the death of Rajiv Ranjan, his wife's one-time boss. Ravi invited him in and asked him to make himself comfortable. Ravi had read about Ranjan's death in the papers.

'Sir, can I ask you when did you last meet the deceased, Mr Ranjan, who died or, maybe I should say, murdered that early morning?' The inspector asked directly. 'Of course, you know about the case, don't you, regarding your wife's ex-boss?'

'It's been a very long time since I saw Mr Ranjan, I think…' Ravi tried to recall.

'Pardon me, sir, but do you know about the argument that took place between your wife and her boss, and the fact that she slapped him? There are stories doing the rounds that she was in a relationship with him. Surely, you know something about it? Because your wife was sacked and had to vacate the company-provided house that you were living in. She is the first suspect. Now, Mr Ravi, try and remember when you last met the deceased.' Ranbir Singh was blunt and did not mince his words.

'It must've been around six months ago,' Ravi said, 'when Mr Ranjan threw a party at the Plaza Hotel. He invited the whole office and some other guests to celebrate his promotion as the director of his company.'

'But why would you say he was murdered?' Ravi continued curiously, 'Everyone believes that it was an accident, a hit-and-run case of a driver who lost control of his vehicle.' He was intrigued.

'Mr Ravi, that is what it might appear to be. But I spoke to two witnesses who say otherwise. They said that the vehicle was a black SUV. One of the witnesses said that he clearly saw that the driver had a black beard. And, both of them said that the driver reversed the car and went over the injured victim a second time. Under such circumstances, an accident takes the shape of a planned murder, which amounts to serious punishment.'

Ravi was shocked. He thought the driver must've lost control of the car and went on the pavement. But this looks like a pre-planned murder. He wondered how Anamika could stoop so low.

He asked the inspector, 'Suppose it was murder, do you have anybody in mind who could have done this?'

'There are a few theories going around. Your wife is the prime suspect. Our theory is that she hired a professional killer and paid him to kill Ranjan, her ex-paramour. So, she didn't have to be in India when the actual killing took place. And she is expected to return to Delhi next week, and we are waiting for her. You are suspected of connivance and conspiracy.'

'Sir,' replied Ravi honestly, 'I have no idea about what happened. I'm in the dark just like you are.'

'Maybe, but you are a suspect. You had a motive to kill someone who had an illicit relationship with your wife. Any husband would carry out an act like this, provided that the husband had some self-respect.' The inspector tried to provoke him.

'What are you talking about? I had no role in this crime, if at all it's a crime. I have absolutely nothing to do with it. You are on the wrong track, if you think that I am involved in this case.'

'No, I am definitely not on the wrong track,' said the inspector. 'The CCTV camera installed on the road reveals the face of the bearded man. He seems like a hardened killer who would take a hefty sum for silencing Ranjan. We also found a tape in Ranjan's locker. The recording, though a bit old, reveals your criminal act in a hit-and-run case many years ago. The victim blackmailed you with it, making your life miserable. Ranjan was not only your wife's lover, but he was also blackmailing you. You have enough reasons to have him killed.'

The inspector continued, handing out an envelope to Ravi, 'Here is a photograph of the killer. Does this ring a bell? Do you know this man? He doesn't have a criminal background though. We have checked the police records. There is nothing.'

Ravi looked at the picture. The face seemed familiar, but he could not place the person. Ravi's face had turned white after hearing about the tape. He quickly composed himself and said, 'No, I don't know him.'

The inspector cleared his throat. He had a habit of doing so before speaking it. 'Hmm, Mr Ravi, here is a fit case. You killed your wife's brother but was not apprehended because you drove away from the scene of the crime. You must've sold the vehicle to someone outside the state, and that's why the police could not trace the Maruti van. Ranjan was blackmailing you and having a relationship with your wife. You see, it's an open-and-shut case. You had all the reasons to kill Ranjan. With one stroke, you would have your revenge.'

'If it isn't a hit-and-run, who could have done such a thing? Who could be behind this ghastly murder?' Ravi asked the inspector, trying to avoid his questioning glance.

Ranbir Singh smiled and said, 'Don't try to change the topic. We studied the case and records in detail. It was either you or your wife. No one else!'

'Why can't it be Suhaila? Ranjan's wife?' asked Ravi. 'She might've had a motive to get her wretched husband killed?'

'Motive to teach a lesson, but not to kill. We had questioned her, and she answered everything. She seems innocent, but not your wife. In fact, both you and your wife could've plotted the murder. That is what the crime branch believes. It seems logical, too. Law is nothing but logic.'

Ravi, though perturbed by the repeated provocation, composed himself. 'That is, actually, not the case. I reiterate that I had nothing to do with Ranjan or his relationship with my wife. You can arrest me or do whatever you want, but it will be futile. I have no idea who hired the killer or, for that matter, who the killer is.'

Inspector Ranbir took a hard look at him, smiled, shook hands and left the house. He purposefully left the photograph on the table. Ravi looked at the picture of the bearded man for a long time, but it did not help.

A few days later, Anamika arrived in Delhi. She was immediately taken in for questioning by the police. She told Ranbir Singh that in Dubai she had spent most of her time in Zayed Hospital, undergoing treatment for depression. But she was silent on the issue of hiring someone to do the job for her. What puzzled the inspector was that her bank account statement did not reveal any cash-withdrawal transaction in the recent past. He was positive that the killer would demand a huge amount of money in return for his services.

When Ravi went to meet Anamika, who was under judicial custody, he met Ranbir Singh who asked him if he knew anything about his wife's bank accounts. Ravi stated matter-of-factly, 'If she had to pay a killer, it isn't necessary that she would withdraw the money from her account. She could have sold her jewellery or even borrowed cash from a friend…'

'…Or from you,' Ranbir finished Ravi's sentence, with an accusing look.

'Why do you keep treating me like a suspect? You know I have nothing to do with this,' said Ravi.

When Ravi met Anamika, he showed her the photograph and asked, 'Who is this man? Do you know him?'

'How would I know him? I have no idea who he is. I've told the police a hundred times. I am innocent. I swear upon my child that I did not pay anyone to kill Rajiv. I swear upon my child, Ravi! I'm telling you the truth. Please believe me.'

'If it's neither you nor Suhaila, then who could it be? You know that I had nothing to do with it. They are suspecting that I hired someone to do the job. They have already proclaimed both of us guilty. When the charges are framed, you and I will be the prime suspects in this gruesome murder.' Ravi was annoyed at being involved in this case just because of a recorded tape.

'Ravi, it isn't up to you to find a solution or solve the case. It's the duty of the police or my lawyer.'

Ravi looked straight into her eyes, but she avoided his glance. Something told him she was lying. 'So, tell me the name of the lawyer you've hired to defend you in court. I'm in this mess as deep as you are. I'd better meet him and seek his advice regarding anticipatory bail.'

Anamika gave him the name of her lawyer—Ramesh Mudgil. 'He had advised me to not speak a word before the crime branch investigation officers,' she said. 'He is a shrewd lawyer. He used to advise my father on various matters. He is reputed to resolve complex cases. He is, what they call, a "legal eagle". He worked as the legal advisor for my company by charging a high retainer fee. Since I had introduced him to Rajiv, he has been indebted to me. So, he agreed to take up my case and help me out of this mess.'

The name pushed Ravi into a flashback. He remembered how that man insulted his father many years ago.

Ravi waited patiently for an hour before Advocate Mudgil

called him to his chamber. Time had taken a toll on the lawyer. His hair had locks of grey now, but Ravi could see that his eyes still had the same shrewd look as before. Senior Advocate Mudgil did not recognize him, which came as a relief to Ravi.

'So, are you Anamika's husband? Ranbir has provided me with first-hand information that he is going to book you for conspiring against Ranjan. Well, what do you have to say to that?' He fired a straightforward question at Ravi in an attempt to rattle him.

Ravi ignored the piercing stare of the shrewd lawyer and asked, 'Mr Mudgil, could you please tell me whether Anamika has really gone this far to orchestrate Ranjan's death?'

'No, no, Ravi, you don't understand. Do you know anything about privileged communication? In accordance with the Advocates Act, 1961, a communication between a lawyer and his client is privileged. Not even the police have the right to raise this question. No, I can't divulge what my client has told me, but I will tell you this—I am going to make sure that she is absolved of this case. I will not let anything happen to her. You need to worry about yourself. Do you want me to prepare an application for an anticipatory bail on a surety bond of ten lakh rupees to bail you out?'

Ravi was at a loss of words at the cunning lawyer. He controlled his anger and continued, 'I am her husband and there is no "privileged communication" when we are discussing the fate of my wife.'

'Sure, Ravi, she is your wife, but she was as close to Ranjan as she is to you, or maybe even more so to the late gentleman,' he winked.

Ravi could not control himself, 'Gentleman? Not at all! A two-timing husband! A dirty, clever, scheming, ruthless blackmailer.'

'What do you mean by "blackmailer"?' Mudgil questioned.

Ravi quickly recovered himself. 'Sorry! That was an unnecessary outburst. I just had to vent my feelings. It's just that I have despised that man from the beginning.'

'I understand, Ravi. That's why I said he was closer to Anamika than you are to her. But let's not waste time on trivial matters. The dead don't come back to tell tales! Just tell me, do you want an application prepared?'

'Yes, please, have the application prepared. And tell me, how do you intend to get us out of the murder charges against us?'

Mudgil had an evil look on his face, 'Money, Ravi, money! Money is the key that opens all doors. Evidence can be manipulated; cops can be bought, and so can the judges. Give me the first instalment of your ten lakhs, and I'll destroy the evidence as well as obtain your anticipatory bail. First, let me see the colour of money, then, I'll tell you my game-plan. I am filing a surety bond of fifty lakhs, along with a bail plea for Anamika.'

Ravi took a deep breath. 'I was unnecessarily dragged into this case.'

'Money, and only money, can save your life now. Anamika, at least, has an alibi. She was in Dubai at the time of the incident, but you were here, and at a place near where Ranjan was found dead. You have no other choice. Get up, arrange the money, and give me the first instalment, or face the dire consequences.'

Ravi could not take it anymore. 'Why do you keep repeating "dire consequences"?'

'When have I repeated it? Are you out of your mind? I just used it for the first time. You are behaving very strangely, Ravi. I suggest that you get up and take action. This meeting is over,' he said, dismissing him.

'Are you sure you'll get us out of troubled waters if the money is delivered?' questioned Ravi, getting up from the cushioned swivel chair.

'Both of your heads are in the lion's mouth, and that lion is Ranbir Singh, a first-rated honest police officer. And I can tell you that the lion firmly intends to bite your heads off. You better watch out, son. Your only hope is Senior Advocate Mudgil, who is skilled and influential enough to get you out of this mess. You should know that smelling a rat and catching one are two different things. Ranbir has smelled a rat, but I will not let him catch it.'

As Ravi was leaving the chambers, he turned back and said, 'I know you will not let your client down, but she is neck-deep in this, so…'

Mudgil flew into a rage and cut him short, 'What do you mean by "neck-deep"? Haven't you heard about the Maria Fernandez murder case? Everyone knows that her stepfather killed her when he found her in a compromising position with their domestic help. He killed both of them and, in privileged communication, he admitted to having committed the gruesome double murder. So, who bailed him out? Senior Advocate Mudgil! No one else could manipulate evidence to this extent. The father was discharged due to the lack of evidence. Who did that? The legal eagle, Advocate Ramesh Mudgil. Do you know that I advised Anamika's father in her brother's case? I saved the entire family from humiliation. So, what if I charged them a hefty fee? I helped the head cashier. Thus, Anamika's father is indebted to me even now.'

Ravi was shocked. 'What about her brother? I have never asked her. Who was the head cashier? What are you talking about?'

'Anamika hasn't told you about her brother? Go and ask her. It's all privileged communication. Now, leave. Don't waste any more of my time.'

Ravi's mind was swirling with questions as he walked out of Mudgil's chamber. What was that about Anamika's brother? What did he mean by the head cashier? How did Mudgil save the entire family from humiliation? But Ravi drew a blank. All he knew was that there was something about Anamika's brother that...

Suddenly, Ravi turned his car around to Anamika's parents' house. He went to the sitting room where the photograph of her late brother hung. He brought it down and compared it with the one of the killer. He was shocked to find that the two were identical. The only thing missing was a beard on the clean-shaven photograph of his brother-in-law.

Ravi rushed to the inspector at the police station with the photograph from the wall. Ranbir Singh called for a beard from his store. The two pictures were identical, except the time they were taken. The two men confronted Anamika who was still in judicial custody. It took a lot of questioning and pressure for her to succumb. She admitted to the crime. She had taken the help of her brother, who lived in Munnar, Kerala. He was working there as a manager at a resort.

Ravi stood in disbelief. Not only had his wife just admitted to having murdered Ranjan, but also to the fact that her brother was never killed. For the past several years, Ravi had been blackmailed for a crime he had not committed. Her brother had survived the accident, but she had ruined Ravi's life anyway. He threw his hands in the air and shouted, 'What kind of a woman are you!'

Inspector Ranbir questioned her, 'If he had survived the accident, how come he had been declared dead by the hospital authorities? And what made him run away and assume another identity? To live in a place like Munnar in hiding?'

Anamika explained in detail, 'My brother, Prashant, was the head cashier at a bank in Chanakyapuri, Delhi. He developed a bad habit of taking cash from the bank's safe to bet on horse races at the Racecourse Ground. One time, he had lost so much money that he could not replace it even if my father had sold everything we had. Prashant would have been sentenced to a period of at least seven years in prison on grounds of embezzlement. That day, while riding the motorbike, his mind was disturbed, and we met with the accident. Both of us were injured. But it was Advocate Mudgil's idea to declare that my brother was brought dead to the hospital, then quietly shift him to a place where he could not be traced. Mudgil manipulated the hospital records and bribed the doctor who attended to my brother. He had a client in Cochin who helped him create a new identity for Prashant. This saved our family.'

Anamika continued, 'Prashant worked a few low-paying jobs in Cochin before joining the resort in Munnar as its assistant manager. When I was dumped by Rajiv for good, I was mad with grief. So, I turned vengeful. I summoned Prashant and convinced him to do this for me. I've always supported him, so he agreed to help me. We believed no one would be able to trace the accident back to him because he lives under a false name. He decided to kill Rajiv by the same method that almost took his life years ago. Only I knew how much I despised Rajiv for what he had done to me. I wanted him dead at any cost.'

Prashant was arrested at his resort in Munnar. A case was filed against him and Anamika. Charges were framed by the crime branch for culpable homicide amounting to murder.

Ranbir Singh met Ravi and said, 'You are in the clear. But

I have a score to settle with Advocate Mudgil. Do you mind if we do a sting operation on him? What you told me about him makes me believe that Ramesh Mudgil is as guilty as his clients are. He is an unscrupulous and ruthless lawyer.'

Ravi was only fourteen when he had begun to despise the man who plunged his family into misery. So, he readily agreed to play the part designed by Ranbir Singh. Carrying a hidden camera, he entered the chamber of the greedy lawyer to give him the ten lakh rupees—supposedly for his bail. He recorded all of Mudgil's boasts about the Maria Fernandez murder case, Anamika's brothers' disappearance, along with other cases he had manipulated.

The recording was handed over to the media. It turned out to be sensational news. The media dug deep and unearthed more incidents of Mudgil's malpractices. Charges were booked against the senior advocate.

∽

Court Room No. 1, a large air-conditioned hall at the Delhi High Court, where Chief Justice Malik and Justice Manohar Dayal presided, was packed with lawyers. Advocate Mudgil pleaded guilty in contempt proceedings against him. The Chief Justice sentenced him to a term of six months behind bars. He was charged a fine of fifty lakh rupees. His licence was revoked. He was disgraced before his own community.

Ravi murmured, 'If you betray your clients and blackmail them, be ready to face the dire consequences.'

For all the help extended by Ravi to solve the case, Inspector Ranbir, after attaining permission from his superiors, returned the tape and erased its existence from the police records.

Ravi sat with his brother, discussing the events of the past several years for the first time. Mohan was shocked. The family had no idea what Ravi had been going through. Taking a deep breath, Mohan said, 'Hatred is a seething, corrosive, adrenalin-pumping intoxicant. It feeds on itself across generations. The divisions of hate do not stop at a target; it finds its way to your door, eventually harming both the hunter and the hunted. Look what happened to them, blackmailing you.'

Ravi nodded in agreement. Mohan put his arm around his younger brother and said lovingly, 'Ravi, put the past behind you. It's time for you to start fresh, with a new chapter.'

Let Me Soar High

A story had to be written about the empowerment of women in India. An unfortunate incident, which came to be known as the 'Nirbhaya case', inspired the authors to write this story about the molestation of a college student in South Delhi. The outline of the story was discussed with Mr Sujoy Mukherjee, son of the legendary actor, the late Joy Mukherjee.

This story has been translated into Hindi by the authors and made into a short film by Joy Mukherjee Productions. The screenplay of the film has also been written by the authors. This short film has won accolades and more than twenty awards at various forums in India and abroad. The film has also won the prestigious Dadasaheb Phalke Award for the 'Best Short Film of 2019' in Mumbai.

At the Jodhpur Film Festival, it has inter alia won an award for the 'Best Story and Screenplay' and is currently making waves at other film festivals in India and abroad.

Devika was in a trance. She was at Vikram's Dance Academy—popularly known as VDA—situated at the basement of a house in Green Park, New Delhi. During her lessons with her instructor Vikram Sehgal, she was always engrossed in the dance. One such day, she did not realize that her batchmates had stopped their practice and were staring at her admiringly, as she completed the routine in perfect synchronization with the Bollywood number playing in the background.

Devika was the daughter of Professor Vijay Khanna—a down-to-earth and righteous gentleman. She was tall, good-looking and full of life, and her lithe figure enhanced her dancing abilities.

She noticed the look in the eyes of her instructor. It was full of admiration. The other fourteen students present at VDA clapped and Devika blushed—embarrassed for having been so carried away. Her neighbour and close friend, Ishita Sabharwal, weighed in, 'You are turning out to be one of Vikram's best students at the academy. And it looks like dancing has become the most important thing in the world to you, that too at such a young age.'

Devika replied, 'I am no longer a child.' She had her birthday coming up in a few days, and then she would become an adult.

Vikram smiled and assured Devika that he was aware of her upcoming birthday on the 24th of January; that she was born at the advent of the new millennium. Devika was astonished to hear that, making her instructor burst out laughing. He then explained that having observed her extraordinary dancing capabilities and the fact that she had not missed a single class; he had sought permission from her father to allow her to participate in the Inter College Dance Festival to be held on the 1st of March at the IGI Stadium, in Delhi. Colleges from all over the country would be participating.

Devika was surprised that no one had mentioned this to her. Vikram told her that her father had granted his permission and had intended to break the news to her on her upcoming birthday. Ishita exclaimed in excitement, 'In case Devika wins, she would get an opportunity to perform at the National Dance Competition held annually in Mumbai. This is fantastic!' Vikram agreed. It was a once-in-a-lifetime opportunity that he was sure Devika would not miss.

Devika was thrilled. She assured her instructor that she would give it her best shot. 'It was, in fact, my father who taught me to put in my best efforts into everything I did,' he said. Since the time she left her Kutub Minar pencil days behind to begin writing with a pen, her father had said to her, 'Things written with a pencil can be erased, but a writing in pen cannot be.' He wanted Devika to also understand that, as she grew older, it would only become more difficult to erase one's mistakes.

After the dance class, Devika and Ishita walked back to their respective homes, one block away. Ishita's excitement continued as she teased her friend, saying that if the latter won, she must give due credit to Vicky. Devika gave her a sharp look and said, 'Vikram is much older to us. He is thirty-three, married and our instructor. Please speak about him with respect.' However, with a little wink, Ishita reminded Devika that she was Vikram's favourite student. Devika wanted to put an end to this teasing, but Ishita continued, placing her hand on her heart, wishing that Vikram was not married.

Devika chided her companion, calling her crazy. 'Vikram is our mentor, and he treats us as his disciples,' she said. 'He always maintains his distance.' Nevertheless, Ishita announced that she wanted him to flirt with her. Both the girls were laughing by the time they reached their block in Green Park. Bidding farewell, they went to their respective buildings.

Shalini, Devika's mother, called out to her daughter the fourth time from the foot of the stairs of their duplex apartment, asking her to get down for breakfast. Finally exasperated, she climbed up the stairs and knocked on her daughter's bedroom door. Devika's music system blared at a high volume, and she was dancing to some latest Bollywood song. Without reducing the volume, she jumped down from her bed and opened the door. Mother and daughter had to scream at the top of their voices to be heard over the music. Devika tried to pull her mother into the room to show her the steps she had been practising. However, Shalini tried reasoning with her. 'You need to study as well. Your dance is not going to get you anywhere. It is not going to help you with your career. And it's time to leave for college now.'

As she walked downstairs, Shalini looked sternly in her husband's direction, who, as usual, was reading the newspaper and sipping his third cup of tea. She told him that it was all his doing. He had given his daughter too much freedom. Prof. Vijay signalled his surrender, throwing his hands in the air, but Shalini was not convinced.

Devika came down in a hurry. She gave her brother a quick hug and said reassuringly to her family that there was no reason for them to worry so much about her. She was a girl of the twenty-first century and could take care of herself. She hugged her father, too, who gave her ₹500 and told her to enjoy herself. He spoke loudly so that his wife would hear him all the way in the kitchen. Laughing whole-heartedly, he told Devika to go and live her life.

Devika was still having her breakfast when a motorbike sounded its loud horn outside. It was her friend from the neighbourhood, summoning her. She rushed through her breakfast, picked up an apple and ran out of the door. She started her scooter and joined Amar, and the two rode together to their college.

As they entered the gates of their college, another friend, Shagufta, greeted them with the good news that the 'Caterpillar' was absent. They were free for the first two lectures. Devika was overjoyed, for it was a relief not having to attend the boring lectures of Mr Talwar, who was nicknamed Caterpillar by the students. She suggested that they go to the college canteen and have coffee. Their other friends would be there, too. She was right. Akhil, Rahul, Aryaman and Nikita were already seated at a table having cold drinks and chatting away.

The vivacious, always ready-for-fun and full-of-life Devika, now proposed to the group that they should bunk the third lecture as well and go to a mall to watch a film. They jumped at her idea. Akhil called out to Charlie, the canteen manager, to cancel their order for burgers, and then the group went off to the Vasant Kunj Mall.

They rushed to the third floor of the mall where the movie theatre was located, pooled money and purchased tickets for a Meryl Streep-starrer *Mamma Mia!*. Amar offered to pay for Devika's share as well, but she refused. They enjoyed the movie, singing along with the songs. Afterwards, they hurried back to college to attend the remaining classes.

Devika celebrated her eighteenth birthday, with all her friends from school and college, at the United Services Institute (USI) in Vasant Vihar. The party continued late into the night. The announcement that Devika had been selected to participate in the Inter College Dance Festival was the main highlight of the event.

Devika began intense preparations for the approaching

competition. She put her heart and soul into her practice, determined to win. She also continued with her college routine, not wishing to fall back on her studies. And often, the group of seven friends met for parties in the evenings as well.

On one such evening, the seven friends—Devika, Amar, Shagufta, Akhil, Rahul, Aryaman and Nikita—were dancing at the No Filters Pub and having a good time, when the DJ stopped the music and made an announcement. The pub was inviting DJ Dias, the renowned DJ from Mumbai, for the Valentine's Day get-together on the 14th of February. 'Those wishing to attend could purchase their passes and food coupons from the counter,' he said.

There was an uproar in the pub. Everybody rushed to get the passes, but Devika and her group had already made other plans. They had bought passes to the Badmaash Company Bar at Cyber City, in Gurugram. They glanced at each other, but before anyone could speak, the DJ spoke into the mic yet again, this time with a request for Devika to perform a dance—the one she had become extremely popular for after an inter-school dance competition. He had been a judge then. Devika obliged as everybody made way for her. She was at the centre of the dance floor with everyone encouraging her, when Ronnie walked into the pub with his bouncers.

Ronnie was the only son of the largest garment exporter in the country. He drove a red Porsche, while his bouncers followed him in an olive-green Hummer. He looked ordinary, with a striking golden streak of colour at the centre of his head. Both his ears were studded with diamond earrings of at least three carats each. His punk-like appearance was not very well liked. He was from the same college and batch as Devika's. He had failed a number of times. The only reason he had not been thrown out of college till now was that his father was a trustee of the college board.

Rahul signalled Devika to stop dancing and she, sensing trouble, quickly joined her friends. Rahul was tall and hefty and provided brotherly protection to his classmates. He was the no-nonsense guy in college and no one messed with him. Other couples took to the floor, and the music started again. Ronnie, who was quite drunk, walked up to Devika and asked why she had stopped dancing. She did not reply. He went nearer and putting his face close to hers, asked again. Devika hurriedly took a step back. By now, Amar and Rahul had stepped up, but before they could stop him, Ronnie held Devika's arm and started pulling her towards the floor. Some pushing and shoving followed as Devika's friends freed her from Ronnie's grip, much to his laughter. Ronnie's bouncers came forward, and the seven friends decided it was better to leave. As they walked out, they could hear Ronnie's voice behind them, shouting above the music that he did not take 'no' for an answer.

It was midnight by the time Devika returned home, and she found her father waiting in the balcony. She had promised to return by 11 p.m. Prof. Vijay pointed at the clock on the wall and reprimanded her. 'You must learn to keep time,' he said. She apologized to him with a hug and climbed the stairs to her room. After the incident at the pub, the friends had had a long talk. They were annoyed with Ronnie's improper behaviour and had decided to avoid him altogether. They did not want any further trouble from him. They had also decided not to mention the incident to anyone, not even their families.

The next day in college, the boys avoided any mention of what had transpired the previous evening, but they noticed that the girls were not over the incident yet. They attended their classes, and after college hours, Devika went for her dance class as usual. As the days passed, she was getting better at her dance performance. She rehearsed her steps to perfection, much to the satisfaction of her instructor.

Devika woke up early on Valentine's Day and switched on her mobile phone, lying next to her pillow. There were already twenty messages from her friends wishing her. She had back-to-back plans with her friends and was excited about the day. That afternoon, the seven friends met at USI. They exchanged greeting cards and gifts with each other. In the evening, they left for Gurugram in Aryaman's Innova, to celebrate the Valentine's Day Special Event. It took a while to reach Cyber City. The traffic had been held up due to the construction of a flyover at Vasant Vihar. Rahul threw his hands in the air showing his frustration. He exclaimed that almost the entire city seemed to be out on the roads.

The party began with a stand-up comedy show by the famous Vir Das. The crowd loved it. They laughed at the comedian's jokes and his mimicry of actors and politicians. The hour-long show went by in no time. Then began the music and dance. It was 11.30 p.m. by the time the food was served. Everyone was hungry after having danced for a long duration. They ate and then headed back home. The seven friends lived in the same area of the city, within a radius of five kilometres from each other. This time Nikhil, being the only teetotaller amongst them, drove the car.

The group in the Innova did not notice the Hummer following them at a distance. They were enjoying themselves, singing and making merry, oblivious to the fact that Ronnie, still furious at Devika for having refused to dance, had decided to teach her a lesson. He had left his own party and was now following them with three of his friends.

Devika and Amar got off at the main gate to their block in Green Park and began walking home. Amar turned into his lane and Devika into hers. She was close to her house when the Hummer that had entered the gates right after the Innova had left, suddenly stopped in front of her. Before she could understand what was happening, Devika saw Ronnie get off the car. He pushed her in, and the Hummer drove towards the basement of the complex.

Devika was shocked. She wanted to scream at the top of her voice, but no sound came from her throat. She was horrified. Ronnie now had his hands on her. She began to struggle, but it was of no use. He ran one hand over her body while capping her mouth with the other. Devika bit his hand sharply and tried to shout for help. The Hummer kept moving around slowly in the basement as Ronnie kissed her on the lips. She struggled to move away, but he overpowered her and pinned her down to the seat. Devika was frantic. All she knew in those moments was that somehow, she had to free herself. Reaching for him, she dug her long nails into his face, causing him to cry out in pain. Ronnie was now furious. He slapped her hard. He now tried to remove her shirt, but failing to do so, tore it off.

Devika was now half-naked and bruised. Her lips had started to bleed. She pleaded with Ronnie to let her go, but Ronnie's drunken head was all out for revenge. He kept yelling, 'You cannot say "no" to me. I will teach you a lesson for saying "no" to me.' He threw her back as she tried to get up, and she hit her head against the door handle. Ronnie shifted, and Devika got her chance. With all her strength, she dug her knee in his groin. He released her, gripping himself with pain. She began screaming for help. She tried opening the door, but it was centrally locked. She started banging on the window, all the while screaming for help. Soon, they heard footsteps approaching, as a security guard came running down into the basement, shouting in response, shining his torch at the Hummer. One of the friends inside the car screamed at the person behind the wheel to drive faster.

Ronnie's friends panicked. They yelled at him to let her go, or all of them would be caught. He realized that they were right, and furiously hit her again. They could now hear other security guards running into the basement, so they slowed down, and opening the door, pushed the half-naked Devika out of the moving car. Two guards at the exit gate tried to stop the vehicle but failed in their attempt. The Hummer could not be stopped by their wooden sticks. Ronnie and his friends sped off down the road.

Prof. Vijay came running down the stairs of his building as soon as he heard about the incident. She was bruised and writhing in pain, as she lay sprawled on the floor of the basement in a semi-conscious state. Soon, other neighbours reached the spot, too, and they helped take Devika up to her house.

When she gained control of herself, Devika saw a sea of grim faces staring at her. The reality of what had happened filled her, and she began to weep bitterly. Shalini took her in her arms to console her. Prof. Vijay wanted to know what had happened, but Devika was unable to speak. No words came out of her mouth. She was shell-shocked.

The neighbours had already called up the police as well as a doctor. Dr Sharma, the neighbourhood physician, came as soon as he could and gave her first aid. Being aware of the procedure in such cases, he advised Prof. Vijay to take his daughter to a hospital for a medical examination.

By now, the police had arrived at the scene. Inspector Rakesh Meena came forward to question Devika, but she still could not speak. Prof. Vijay and Shalini helped her control herself and comforted her so that she could give details to the police. She spoke, crying as she did, of how Ronnie had forced her into his car and had molested her. Devika managed to go over what had happened. She told the inspector that there were three other boys with Ronnie. She did not know their names. She relived the incident as the inspector recorded her statement. When she had finished, the police officer addressed her parents and said that she would have to go through a medical examination. It was mandatory to confirm her declaration.

Rohit was informed of what had happened. He joined his family at the trauma unit of the All India Institute of Medical Sciences, where the examination was carried out. The medical report confirmed that Devika had been subjected to sexual abuse. The Khanna family shuddered to think of what may have happened had the security guard not heard Devika's calls. Inspector Rakesh Meena now assured them of his complete cooperation in booking the accused. He would book the culprits under the requisite sections of the Indian Penal Code and see to it that they were sent behind bars. He immediately gave the orders, and his officers were dispatched to nab the accused.

Devika was taken home. She was extremely disturbed. She was injured not only physically, but mentally as well, and it felt as if the traumatic experience would stay with her throughout her life. She had to be given sedatives so that she could sleep.

The next morning, Prof. Vijay and Rohit, along with some neighbours, went to the police station. They received a rude shock when they realized that though a case had been registered for sexual harassment, voluntarily causing injury and criminal intimidation, it was not against Ronnie. The case was registered against Rajendra, one of Ronnie's drivers. Ronnie's name was not even mentioned in the First Information Report.

The whole case had been falsified. Prof. Vijay understood that Ronnie's father had flexed his muscle and money power. He had manipulated the entire incident by creating circumstantial evidence that Ronnie, who had a party that same night, had never left his farmhouse. It was the handiwork of his driver, who was in Green Park that night to drop off a guest. He had seen Devika and pulled her into the Hummer. The facts had been changed to fiction, and the entire case had no trace of Ronnie.

Inspector Meena was also a changed man. He told Prof. Vijay that the police had recorded Ronnie's statement. The latter was at his own party till 3.15 a.m. when the last of his guests left his farmhouse. Several of his friends had vouched for that fact. Further, the inspector said that Devika, being drunk, had mistaken the driver Rajendra for Ronnie.

Prof. Vijay could barely control his anger. Rohit immediately held his hand and asked him to restrain himself. Prof. Vijay felt extremely helpless and disappointed. He tried to convince the inspector that his daughter had not been drunk; so she could easily distinguish between two people. He appealed to the inspector to understand that this was all a cover-up. But all his appeals were in vain. Inspector Meena's reply was simply that the police operated on evidence and not on hearsay.

Rohit could not control himself any longer. He asked the inspector what more was needed when the security guards of the block had also witnessed what had transpired in the basement. That was clinching evidence in itself. Not wanting any further questions, the inspector rose from his seat. Looking at the father and son, he told them that they ought to be grateful that it was only a case of molestation, not rape. Prof. Vijay and Rohit were shocked. They could only stare at the inspector as he walked away. But they could do nothing except return home. Once he realized that the police were not inclined to help, Prof. Vijay decided to seek legal advice from a lawyer. He realized that it would be an uphill task for him to get justice from a corrupt system.

Devika, meanwhile, had gone numb. She had neither eaten nor spoken since waking up. Salini's attempts at comforting her were of no help. Shalini had also informed Devika's friends, and they were all with Devika now, but even their presence did not ease the tension. Amar was visibly distraught because he could not understand how, within minutes of his leaving his dear friend, such a ghastly incident had occurred. She was unmoved by their repeated attempts to start a conversation. Nothing they did cheered her up.

Soon, Devika started showing signs of anxiety. She told her mother to ask everyone to leave. She could not stand the inquisitive questions and the steady stream of visitors any more. All of a sudden, she got up and went into the washroom, locking the door behind her. She stepped into the tub and stood under the shower. Streams of water came pouring down on her. She tried to scrub away in all the places where Ronnie's hands had touched her, without realizing that she had not even undressed. She rubbed herself fiercely with soap and began crying hysterically. Filling the tub with water, she lay down in it, trying to hold her breath. She wanted to end it all. She wanted to remove the memory of Ronnie once and for all. But she could not carry it through. Despair overtook her, and she began banging her head on the washroom wall.

After some time, there was commotion outside the bathroom door. Prof. Vijay, Shalini, Rohit and her friends were calling out her name, asking her to come out. Scared that she would harm herself, they kept telling her everything would be alright. Finally, to everyone's relief, Devika opened the door.

But, this incident had alarmed the family terribly. So, Prof. Vijay asked his mother—Devika's grandmother—to come and stay with them. They did not wish to leave Devika alone in the house. Dadi, as Devika called her, would be with her whenever Shalini needed to step out.

In the days that followed, Devika remained in her own room, not wishing to speak to anyone. She barely ate. She refused to go to college or even to her dance class. She stayed wrapped up in her agony, not sharing it with anyone. The family had received news that the police had arrested Ronnie's driver. They concluded that being poor, the man must have accepted a lot of money for taking the blame for Ronnie. Prof. Vijay, Shalini and Rohit were helpless. As much as they wanted to see the culprit punished, they could do nothing.

Amar, Shagufta, Akhil, Rahul, Aryaman and Nikita visited Devika often, but she barely spoke to them. They would call her up only to be told that she was not in the mood to talk. She refused to go out of the house or make any plans with them. The whole household seemed to have come to a standstill. An uneasy silence had replaced the usual laughter, conversation and just general noises that otherwise tinkled through the house. Devika's presence was terribly missed though she was always in the house now. The family longed for the old carefree and fun-loving girl, who was forever running in and out of the house, making plans, running up and down to her room and filling the house with her lively presence. Often both Dadi and

Shalini would chew over why it had to be their little girl to have had to go through such an experience.

One afternoon, the doorbell rang. Vikram, the dance instructor, walked in along with Devika's friend Ishita. His eyes burned with anger. He had only now heard of the incident and had come rushing to see Devika. His expression was full of concern for his student, whom he genuinely liked. Devika's mother called her downstairs to the living room. Devika was surprised to see her instructor but was still not ready to talk about the harrowing and frightening experience that she had gone through. Understanding her state, he said he did not wish to disturb her but asked her to hear him out.

The instructor explained to her that it was important for her to try and distract herself. He insisted that she must slowly try to get back to her regular routine and participate in the Inter College Dance Festival. But Devika was not ready to go out of the house yet, not even to attend college. She was not ready to face the way people might look at her or the comments they might pass. And worst of all, she was not ready to face Ronnie, who would be there. She also informed Vikram about the driver being taken into custody, and how the police had done nothing but side with the rich and powerful. The thought that Ronnie was roaming around free had Devika crying again.

Vikram said, 'If you continue to sulk, you are just letting Ronnie and his friends win. You need to get out of your bedroom, begin your practice and compete in the festival.' He said he wanted to see her rise like the sun, work harder than ever before, and show the world her true mettle. Vikram reminded Devika that she was a unique person with enormous talent and that she should only focus on that, he concluded. Vikram's words of wisdom encouraged Devika. When he got up to leave, he extracted a promise from her that she would join the dance classes next month.

After about a week, Devika started to involve herself in completing her course. The examinations were approaching, and she did not want to miss them and waste a year.

Her shortfall in attendance was excused by the principal. Devika appeared for the papers and just about cleared them. She dreaded the sight of Ronnie, who made it a point to come close to her and smile, as though to tell her that in spite of everything, nothing had happened to him. He had managed to get away without a scratch. This continued to frustrate Devika.

Once the examinations were over and the holidays began, Devika went back to staying at home. She seemed to have lost a taste for celebrations. She preferred being a recluse. There was no dancing, no shopping, no movies and parties, and no extracurricular activities. She seemed to have forgotten her life before the incident.

Shalini and Devika's grandmother took her to a psychiatrist for counselling. He had a heart-to-heart talk with her and suggested that Devika keep herself busy by engaging in some activity or the other. Staying engrossed would help her distract herself from what had happened to her on the night of 14th February.

Shalini thought that a change of scene might help her daughter. She packed Devika's bags and sent her to her sister's house in Chandigarh. It was a huge bungalow with a kitchen garden and even a small swimming pool in the backyard. Shalini was sure Devika would enjoy her stay there. Her relatives, especially her cousin sister, took good care of Devika, but she remained aloof and quiet. She seemed to have forgotten how to laugh or even smile.

After a month, when Devika returned to Delhi after her holidays, she requested her parents to change her college. Rohit, realizing that her discomfort was regarding Ronnie, asked her if she had not been informed about him. He had met with an accident and was seriously injured. He was lucky to have survived but sustained multiple fractures all over his body. He would need four months or more to walk properly. Rohit could not help but smile at his sister. He said nothing more but his expression said it all. Ronnie finally got the punishment that was due to him. It was then that Devika's face lit up with her old smile, after a gap of months. She began to attend college regularly.

One evening, Prof. Vijay suggested that Devika joined her dance class. She had promised Vikram that she would, but had not. He also recommended that she began going out with her friends like she used to. Shalini supported him, as she too wanted Devika to resume dancing and do the things she enjoyed the most. But she was apprehensive about how Devika would get around. Prof. Vijay said, 'It should be the way she had gone around earlier—on her scooter. The sooner Devika was back on her feet and lived her earlier life, the better. It was time for her to get back to being normal.' The grandmother intervened. She was not sure why her son was pushing her granddaughter after all that had transpired. 'What are you trying to prove?' she asked him. The father did not want her past to destroy her from inside. He did not want that his daughter should bow down to the way men in society thought—that women were puppets. Devika would follow her dreams and soar high.

Her father's words hit her, and Devika once again joined the classes at VDA. Her instructor took particular care of her to make her feel comfortable. In fact, he had a soft corner for her, but maintaining the dignity of the guru–disciple relation, he never crossed its boundaries. He paid special attention and showered Devika with more than the required praise, just to boost her sagging morale. But Devika found it agonizing to dance amongst the other students. She was always conscious of the fact that they knew about her past. She knew that she was not at fault but the whole incident had traumatized her and had made her doubt herself.

Vikram began preparing her for the Inter College Dance Festival that Devika had missed the previous year. It was held annually on the 1st of March at the IGI Stadium in Delhi. The competition was two months away, and Vikram was sure that with some practice, she would be ready for it. Gradually, Devika began to attend her classes regularly, and her old life seemed to come back to her.

A day before the competition, Vikram took her to rehearse at the IGI Stadium. Devika danced well, and her instructor was extremely satisfied with her performance. He was satisfied with himself, too, and heaved a sigh of relief. His best student was ready.

The next day, Devika reached the stadium with her instructor and other dancers at 3.30 p.m. The competition was to begin at 5 p.m. A big crowd of college students had already gathered, and Devika felt a chill run down her spine. She asked herself whether she would be able to perform in front of the large crowd expected that evening. Sensing her nervousness, Vikram patted her shoulder and said, 'You will be all right. You are the best.'

Devika's solo dance performance was scheduled for 6 p.m. She appeared on the stage, trying to remain confident and at ease. But when she started to dance, she spotted Ronnie in the front row, staring at her. Suddenly, she was overwhelmed, and she fell down. She tried to get up, but couldn't. Ronnie's presence made her feel nervous and tears trickled down her cheeks.

The music continued to play, but she found it difficult to get on her feet. Her knees had gone weak. Devika heard her instructor's voice over the loud music.

Vikram stood at the wings of the stage calling out to Devika, 'Get up' Devika! Get up! Gather all your strength and get up! You can do it!' Devika mustered all her strength and slowly got back on her feet. And then, she began to dance.

She danced as she had never danced before. Her feet moved on the floor as if somebody had electrified them. Her performance seemed to have a spark of divinity to it. The audience presumed that her fall was a part of the performance. When she finished, there was deafening applause. She was declared the best dancer in the competition. Her relatives and friends were overjoyed.

A cash prize of five lakh rupees awaited her, and so did the next step of participating in the National Dance Competition in Mumbai. Moreover, Devika was offered a modelling assignment by one of the biggest advertising companies in India. The old Devika was back.

In spite of all that she had endured, she had put the past behind her by choosing to fly with her dreams and soar high.

Masqueraders from the North

It is a real-life story about a certain placement agency, which played a fraud on innocent and naive farmers from Punjab. The poor farmers were compelled to sell off their lands on being lured to high paying jobs in the Middle East and Canada. The owners of the placement agency later closed all of their establishments and vanished.

The story also sends a stern message to the people of the north-western belt of India to not to fall prey to the guiles of such unscrupulous manpower suppliers who lure poor farmers and fleece them after giving false hopes of jobs abroad.

A tall, turbaned and rugged-looking Sikh stood at the edge of a hilly terrain, facing the vast sea. His facial expression reflected tranquillity, as though he had just attained his heart's desire. He stood there for some time enjoying the view of the shimmering waves flowing gently on to the white beach of Fujairah in the United Arab Emirates. It was a dream come true. The achievement of securing work in the UAE gave him immense satisfaction and excitement.

He—along with his sixty co-workers—had finally arrived in this country, all the way from Punjab in India. The placement agency that he had come through had secured employment for him with a construction company, for a handsome salary. He had been overjoyed and had shared the news with his family with a triumphant look on his face.

He had to argue, cajole and finally convince his parents to sell a piece of agricultural land owned by them so he could pay the placement agency. His parents had initially resented selling the only asset they owned. They were relying on it to arrange for his younger sister's dowry for when they would eventually get her married, but he had used all his emotional skills to convince them otherwise. He had reasoned that once he started working as a carpenter in a Dubai-based construction company, he would be able to earn so much money that all their debts, problems and miseries would end. He could also get his sister married lavishly. This barren piece of land was nothing in front of the huge earnings that he would make in Dubai.

As he stood there within the boundary wall of Fujairah Hotel looking at the Arabian Sea, Sardar Ajit Pal Singh said a silent prayer of gratitude, continuing to inhale the fresh air. The year was 1995, and massive structural development was taking place in the UAE. After the renovation assignment currently in progress at the hotel, the construction workers were to be sent to Dubai to render their services at an upcoming mall at Sheikh Zayed Road. That was what the new Arab employers told the incumbents, who paid the placement agency through their noses to get a job in the UAE.

All the sixty-one workers were from Punjab, mostly uneducated Sikhs or Punjabi-Hindus. They had applied to the Star Placement Agency's advertisement two months ago, that appeared on the *Punjab Times*—a newspaper published in the vernacular and popular in the entire state. Each one of them had collected ₹5 lakhs—many with the help of their parents, either through selling assets or by using up all their savings—to pay the agency.

They were told that Fujairah was an Emirate on the east coast of UAE, opposite the Indian coast. It lay along the Gulf of Oman and was known for its pristine beaches and the Al-Hajar Mountains. The agency had promised to give them a tour of all the famous places, such as Wadi Wurayah, RAK Zoo and Al Hayl Castle, once their work in Fujairah was completed. They were to work on a trial basis and receive their first remuneration in dirhams, amounting to about ₹1 lakh, once they were in Dubai. They had agreed to this proposal.

The accommodation of the workers was arranged in the dormitory of the hotel. They were grateful to the agency for taking complete responsibility in transporting them from Ludhiana to Bombay and then from there by a cargo ship to Fujairah. They were also provided assistance with filling up the UAE visa forms, as most of them knew only Gurmukhi, their native language. Ajit Pal was the only one who had been to primary school and could understand a little bit of English, and this gave him an edge over the other uneducated men. It made him the most confident in the group. He told his companions that the remuneration for the work they had done in Punjab would seem like peanuts compared to the dirhams they would receive in the UAE.

Ajit Pal spotted Maninder Singh, also known as Mani, running towards him, waving a letter in his hand. Mani was his friend and neighbour from Phillaur District, his hometown in Ludhiana, Punjab. Having made full use of the hotel letterhead that fascinated him, he had just written a letter to his parents informing them of his safe arrival. Ajit Pal smiled as he looked at his friend who seemed different already. He had been a dejected and depressed youth, with no source of income when they had gone to the office of the agency in Ludhiana. Just two months back, he seemed to have no aim in life and seldom smiled. Today, he seemed vivacious and beaming with confidence.

Maninder asked Ajit Pal excitedly whether he had written to his parents. They would be worried after all. He held out the paper in his hand and showed Ajit Pal the gold-embossed imprint of the hotel. He could not understand the Arabic script, but that did not matter. He was completely taken in by its beauty.

'What matters is that we are in Fujairah, and in a few days we will be in Dubai,' Mani exclaimed, smiling.

The two walked back to the hotel where their companions were working in the ground floor hall. Some of them waved, big smiles on their faces. They had their letters too. These were to be given to Neeraj Kumar, co-owner of Star Placement Agency. Neeraj's wife, Malini headed the agency.

A few days passed. The labourers worked day and night within the hotel premises under the supervision of Pran Kohli, an architect. The hotel, spread over an area of four acres, had a congenial working atmosphere because though the men remained indoors, they were a happy and enthusiastic lot. Soon, Ajit Pal's restlessness took over him. He was curious and wanted to go out of the hotel premises. He wanted a feel of the surrounding area. He had never been out of India or even heard of a place called Fujairah. He had no knowledge of what it looked like. The little information they had about it was what the agency had given them. He wanted to get acquainted with this foreign land.

With the thought of looking around, he walked towards the exit, but the security guards at the main gate stopped him from going out without Neeraj's permission. Ajit Pal felt dejected. But he waited patiently till the next day when he could speak to Neeraj. The latter scolded the guards for their behaviour and told Ajit Pal he could definitely go out of the premises, but he was not to venture too far as they were in a foreign land. He also asked him to avoid speaking with the local people for they were easily offended.

After Neeraj left, Ajit Pal walked out to see the area around. A security guard, who had been ordered to keep an eye, followed at a distance, unnoticed. The hotel was situated in a secluded expanse, with barely any habitation around. At a distance, Ajit Pal saw a small house-like structure and out of curiosity, walked towards it. A dark-skinned man in a drunken state sat on a chair just outside the main entrance. He had a table by his side on which lay a plate of fish curry and a glass half-filled with some liquid.

Ajit Pal was curious and decided that a little conversation would be harmless. 'Indian or Arab?' he enquired.

The man replied with a thick English accent, 'Very much Indian.'

Ajit Pal thanked his lucky stars. The first person he had met turned out to be an Indian. He asked, pointing towards the west, 'Is Dubai on the other side?'

'Yes,' the man replied.

Ajit Pal noticed that the Indian was quite drunk, and he had disturbed him by this sudden interchange of dialogue. He walked on, looking around for a short while, and then he retraced his steps to the hotel. He shared this little adventure with his co-workers and told them about the man he had met, who had confirmed that Dubai was on the other side of the sea. Broad smiles were exchanged. In a few minutes, all the workers had been transmitted the news of them being close to Dubai. They thanked the placement agency and its good-looking directors who had been extremely nice to them. Neeraj and Malini were fluent in speaking Arabic as they spoke in the same language with the owners of the hotel whom the workers were serving. Neeraj and Malini were tall, good-looking and articulated themselves quite well. They were impressive, to say the least.

A month of hard work had passed. Ajit Pal, once again, began to long for the outside air. He expressed his desire to explore more. After all, they were in a foreign land, and he must know more about it, he thought. As he walked past the house-like structure, he saw the dark-skinned man once again. He sat on the same chair as before, but this time he was sipping coffee. Seeing him sober, Ajit Pal thought it would be a good chance to increase his knowledge of the place. Nodding a greeting, he asked the man about the places to visit in Fujairah.

The man looked at him curiously, 'What place are you talking about?'

'Fujairah.'

'I have never heard of such a place in this area.'

Ajit Pal gave a perplexed look. The dark man stared back at him, a bit confused.

'We are working at that hotel,' said the Sikh, pointing in the direction. 'We came here about a month ago. My name is Ajit Pal.'

'So, how can I help you? Tell me, friend.'

Ajit Pal asked the man if he knew Hindi and when he replied that he did, he immediately spoke in the language he was more comfortable expressing himself in.

'Sir, I just wanted to know the popular places to visit here in Fujairah. Our placement agency has brought us from India to work here in the UAE.'

The man laughed at this. Ajit Pal could only stare at him,

but he started feeling that something was amiss.

'What, man? What do you mean, Fujairah? No, no, no, this is not Fujairah. This is not the UAE. This is India. You are in Goa, and that hotel shut down a long time back. It was known as Goa Beach Resort. This is Taluka Bardez, man. Reis Magos area of Goa. Who told you that you were in the UAE? What, man!'

Ajit Pal had the shock of his life. He was dumbfounded.

The dark man continued in Hindi, 'This place is near the Three Kings Church, man! In Taluka Bardez near Panjim. The river that flows into the Arabian Sea is the Mandovi river. I don't know about Fujairah, but Dubai is certainly on the other side of the sea, my friend. You are in Goa. Very much in India!'

He was still laughing as Ajit Pal walked away. The Sikh felt as though he would sink in the sand. He felt sick as it began dawning upon him that they had been tricked and cheated by the placement agency. They had never crossed the Indian border. The visas, the renovation work—everything was a ruse.

The Arabs moving around the hotel compound were as fake as an actor doing a beggar's role. It dawned on him that the letterheads in Arabic, the hoardings placed in the hotel at strategic points displaying the malls of Dubai, they were all a part of the grand plan to dupe the sixty-one workers. He felt like strangling the owner of the placement agency with his bare hands.

∞

In the bungalow, while the preparations were on in full swing, the chain by which the extraordinary crystal chandelier hung came loose. As the piece, embedded with three thousand crystals, began to drop towards the floor, the waiters and helpers held their breath. Suddenly, out of nowhere, a figure leapt forward to grab the chain. Using all his strength, he was able to prevent an imminent crash. The chandelier hung just two feet above the Italian marble floor. Everyone applauded at the heroic feat shown by Neeraj. He had used not only his physical strength and agility but also his presence of mind to save the expensive piece of artistic beauty from falling down. Moreover, he had also prevented at least a few people from being injured.

Neeraj, and his beautiful wife Malini, were preparing for a lavish party to be held that same evening at their accommodation, situated near Candolim Beach in Goa. The couple had just moved to Goa a few days back. They had taken this sprawling bungalow on rent from its owner, Pran Kohli. It had a breathtaking view of the Arabian Sea, and that had been the deciding factor. A cheque for ₹6 lakhs, as security, had been given to Pran Kohli, who had held it in awe.

Neeraj and Malini made a striking couple. They were in the placement business. They had extended invitations to the elite of Goa, through their contacts, but had not anticipated that the arrangements would take so long to be carried out. Just when everybody was running helter-skelter, and everything was in full gear to complete the work in progress, the chandelier had come loose. However, it was restored to its original position, and the work resumed.

The whole look of the place was one of extravagance. An S-Class black Mercedes-Benz, parked in the garage, lent further credence and glitter to the riches of the couple, who, apart from the agency, also owned two hotels, one each in New Delhi and Jaipur.

'It would indeed turn out to be an evening to remember,'

whispered Malini in her husband's ear, with a mischievous gleam in her eyes.

'Yes, of course!' He replied with excitement, 'and the stupid bugger would be our next victim.' Both of them laughed.

He went on to state with arrogance, 'The liquor displayed alone is worth two lacs, and the food has been arranged from the best caterers in Panjim. Goans are fond of good food and liquor. You win over one, you win over them all, and then we will strike.'

Malini nodded in agreement. They winked at each other and returned to finish their preparations for the party with a smile on their faces.

Malini, who was well versed with arranging lavish get-togethers, was sure that her invitees would be pleased. Later that evening, the thirty-five elite guests that arrived, led by the influential former minister Dilip Konkar, were more than just pleased. They were mesmerized by the extravagant show managed by the charming Malini. She, along with her husband, welcomed them and played the role of the perfect hostess.

Live music—played by the Diaz Band—set the tone for the evening. The invitees enjoyed themselves thoroughly as the drinks, and the delicious snacks made the rounds. Malini took the mic in her hands to address her guests, who were more than eager to listen to her. She told them about the time she and Neeraj had spent in America and London and how they had come to India after a long stint abroad. The audience was captivated. She stated that in India, they had land holdings in Delhi and Jaipur and now intended to purchase one in Goa, too. She spoke in impeccable English, uttering many praises for the Goan people and their beautiful state. She stated, rather modestly, that she and her husband had a budget of five crores.

The guests were immensely impressed.

Malini, having made her mark, further stated that they owned several hotels and real estate businesses in the US, Canada, the UAE and the UK. They had a list of esteemed clients. Moreover, their company, headed by her, took pride in their staff that was very talented and had the requisite skills, which any multinational company needed to flourish. Malini articulated herself perfectly while most of the Goans gulped down a couple of drinks.

The party continued till the wee hours of the morning, and the last guest to leave was Dilip Konkar. The occasion was a grand success. Malini and Neeraj had arrived in Goa in style. Most of them had left in an inebriated form with a smile on their lips.

Neeraj had prior information that the former minister, Dilip Konkar, was a rich businessman and had two hotels in Goa—one at Vagator and the other at Reis Magos, near Coco Beach—but there was something shady about him. No one trusted him as he never honoured his commitments. Malini and Neeraj, nevertheless, paid him a visit, with a proposal. They offered to buy Goa Delights, an old hotel owned by him, which, at present lay under the lock and key of the Economic Development Corporation in Panjim—a government organization that provided finance to businessmen for promoting tourism in Goa. Dilip Konkar owed the Corporation ₹2.60 crores. Malini and Neeraj offered to pay him four crores for the hotel as an outright purchase. The offer made the politician think. After settling his debt, he would make a clean profit of ₹1.40 crores. His mind raced towards the utilization of the extra money that he would get from their proposal.

Malini was beyond beautiful. There was something about

her that fascinated people. She had sharp features, a good height and a voluptuous body that many men dreamed about. Konkar, in a few minutes into the meeting, was addressing Malini more than Neeraj, to the amusement of the latter.

In the next meeting, their third, Malini threw all her charm on Konkar. She complimented him for his Goan sensibility, his intellect and his attractive looks. He was not like other men, and that was why she liked him, she said. All this was said before Neeraj walked in, when Malini, to Konkar's surprise, changed the topic. Neeraj gifted Konkar an expensive Rolex wristwatch and a gold necklace to his wife. Besides, he also offered him ₹10 lakhs in cash as earnest money towards the purchase of his property. Konkar was not a person to accept a proposal by two strangers as early as in their third meeting. He accepted the gifts gladly but refused to take the money.

Konkar did not know that Malini was not the kind to take a refusal. She convinced him to accept the money, without even issuing a receipt to them. It was inauspicious for them to take the money back, she said. In a few days, if he decided not to enter into a deal with them, he could return the money. Konkar was impressed by the courteous, glamorous and seductive Malini. He was overawed that she would leave ₹10 lakhs with him without a receipt, just like that. No written commitment of any kind. What he did not realize then was that it was all bait.

Malini had taken his hand in hers and looked straight into his eyes. Neeraj had excused himself from the room. She took every opportune moment she could to seduce Konkar, and he fell for it.

After a few days, Malini invited the Konkars over to her house in Candolim. Konkar deliberately did not pass on the message to his wife, and when he arrived at Malini's lavishly furnished home, he was pleased to find her alone. She offered him a drink and discussed everything from politics to her experiences in Dubai, Mauritius and Switzerland. As usual, she looked so beautiful that Konkar heard only half of what she said. His mind was elsewhere. He was comparing her to his wife and desired more than ever, to befriend her. Malini's actions and her long stares at him only added to his desire. Malini was very good-looking and with each passing moment, he longed for Malini more and more.

He fell for her and decided to accede to her proposal of going ahead with selling Goa Delights to her. In fact, he agreed with whatever Malini said after that. He wanted to get as close as possible to this charming woman and would do whatever she demanded of him. He had fallen head over heels for her.

Much to Konkar's dismay, Neeraj's arrival disrupted the starry-eyed exchange they were having. He felt annoyed with Neeraj for walking in at a crucial moment and hoped that he would leave, but that was not to be. Neeraj went into the adjacent room and brought out two bags in style. Each contained ₹20 lakhs in cash, and he presented these to Konkar. The freshly printed, neatly stacked notes looked very appealing. The greed glittered in Konkar's eyes. He took the bags and executed a receipt-agreement that was magically produced from a closet by Malini. He signed it without reading a word. He completely overlooked the clause that stated that the possession of his hotel was being handed over to Neeraj and Malini on his acceptance of ₹50 lakhs out of the agreed sum of ₹4 crores. He just signed the document while glancing at Malini from time to time.

Neeraj told him that a copy of the receipt-agreement would reach him the next day. Dilip Konkar, for the first time in his life, had behaved entirely out of character. He was completely smitten by Malini and wished to oblige her in every possible way.

Two days later, Malini invited the Konkars to lunch at a Bagga Beach restaurant, and there she presented them with expensive gifts. It made the Konkars feel on top of the world, and they enjoyed the meal thoroughly. The next evening, Neeraj visited the Konkars' with a diamond necklace for Mrs Konkar. The gifts were pouring in, and for the first time in his life, Dilip Konkar was compromising his principles. He had always been the hunter, but now he was the prey. He was neck-deep in debt and found himself accepting cash and expensive gifts one after the other, from a couple he had only recently met. Yet, he could not, or did not, stop himself. Instead, he was on cloud nine. He believed all his problems would end now. His greed and wicked intentions were making him do the impossible, and he began to believe that very soon, he would have the best of both worlds—enough wealth and a beautiful woman by his side. He even forgot to ask for the copy of the signed agreement and believed whatever Malini said.

A few days later, Neeraj and Malini went over to the Konkars with a request. Neeraj told them that his parents, who were in London, were coming to Goa to visit them, and they wished to see the hotel he and Malini were buying. Malini asked very sweetly if they could have the keys to the property. On seeing Konkar's hesitation, they told him that they wanted to employ labourers to renovate the old, dilapidated hotel at their own expense. Konkar asked for more payment. Neeraj took out his chequebook and asked Malini to sign a leaf for two crore rupees. He then handed it over to Konkar. A single check of such a large amount, issued in an instant, had the latter overwhelmed yet again. Neeraj looked at Konkar's bewildered expression and explained to him that Malini belonged to a royal family. She had received an enormous inheritance—a huge bank balance, properties and jewellery. He was more of an employee of Malini's. They laughed, Malini blushed a little, and Konkar relaxed.

Malini reached for her handbag and took out some ornaments. They were on their way to deposit the treasure in a newly opened bank locker, she said. The Konkars gaped. The diamond and other precious-stones embedded jewellery were the finest they had ever set their eyes on. 'Three hundred years old,' Neeraj informed the Konkars. He went on to say that, his wife was so generous that once she had gifted such an expensive piece of jewellery to a sheikh in Dubai. Dilip Konkar could not take it anymore. He immediately sprang up, fetched the hotel keys and handed them over to Malini. He wondered whether one day he would be lucky enough to receive one such ancient piece of art, that too from the hands of Malini.

Konkar was feeling great. Since he had met the couple, his boring and monotonous life had taken a complete turn. There was a whiff of money, and of a romance brewing between him and the beautiful Malini. Pandit Ramdev was absolutely right when he had predicted that his misery and sorrow was going to end very soon and that he would be ushered into a life that would bestow upon him so much money, affection and love. He would soon show everyone who had insulted him and considered him a 'has been', that he was back at the helm of the affairs.

He was sitting and having a beer with his close friend Ganesh Perulekar and boasting about his smart moves, when Perulekar cautioned him, 'Konkar, don't you think everything seems a little too good, too hunky-dory? I somehow smell a rat here. I think everything that is happening is just too good to be true.'

Konkar was not to be discouraged. 'Oh, Peru! You are just jealous of me. I have hit the bull's eye. Why don't you understand? I have given her nothing but have taken so much. A few days back only she gifted my wife a diamond necklace worth a fortune.' He continued, this time with disgust, 'I do not know whether it will look good on my wife, but it would definitely go with Malini's personality.'

He went on, 'You do realize that the necklace is an expensive one and rarely would anybody gift such a necklace to a person that they have met just a few days back. You will never ever understand, my dear Peru, she is not only gorgeous but has a heart made of gold. She is so nice, so beautiful, so charming. Oh, Peru! I am in love with her and would do anything for her,' his voice rose to a higher pitch as he became emotional.

Peru was a good friend and a sensible one at that, 'But tell me, Konki, why would she select you out of the lot? Philips and Sadashir Prabhu are more influential and smarter. Why, of all people, would she choose you, unless she had some ulterior motive? Don't go ahead blindly and jump into deep water from where you can't swim back to the shore. Beware, my friend, when someone is sweet and over-friendly, there has to be a catch.'

'See, I told you, you are jealous of my achievements and want me to remain a puppet tied to strings and keep following Sadashir Prabhu as an assistant. No, I will totally overshadow each one of these good-for-nothing fellows. I will laugh at their swollen faces. I am very soon going to receive my balance payments, and I will be as rich as I used to be, before I lost my money in gambling. I will beat these guys hands down, and mark my words, when I will be seen at the Azul at Cidade with Malini, the so-called friends of ours will be surprised.'

He continued, 'Peru, those days are not far when I will rule the city. If you want me to be cautious and miss this opportunity, you have another thing coming your way. Not me, man, I am going places with Malini by my side.'

He had no intentions or inclinations to look deeply into the matter. 'You are not thinking wisely. One day, you shall repent that you did not adhere to my advice, dear friend,' said Perulekar.

After having his fill of grilled fish, Perulekar left to meet his friend, Police Inspector Tambe, who was posted at the Police Headquarters in Panjim. He had decided to discuss these 'too good to be true' happenings that revolved around Malini, taking the Goans by storm.

He drove his old second-hand Fiat and pondered over the recent state of events, 'Was he in the wrong?' It was 2003; there were people from Mumbai, Bengaluru and Delhi who were showing interest in real estate in Goa. Tourists had started visiting Goa even during the monsoons, which was unheard of. Some hotels that would close down from April to September had started giving monsoon packages. But he still decided to go ahead and speak to Tambe about this couple who had come out of nowhere and got so many Sikhs working in the hotel under the supervision of two Arabs, who were dressed in the traditional white robes. What was happening inside the hotel?

Konkar had mentioned that he had not given possession of the property to Neeraj and Malini, but just allowed them to do a little bit of renovation. 'Well,' he spoke aloud, 'Why should there be so many workers to renovate the hotel just so that it could be shown to Malini's parents.' Something certainly seemed fishy.

He crossed over the Mandovi Bridge and took a right turn towards the Police Headquarters—the famous, old Portuguese yellow-coloured building that housed the law enforcement agencies. He found a parking space in front of Bombay Bazaar and started walking towards the police headquarters to discuss this issue with his friend, Inspector Anil Tambe.

While walking down the road, he felt dizzy, and his knees trembled a bit. Perulekar fell down, and later when he opened his eyes, he found himself in the Apollo Hospital at South Goa. He had been diagnosed with Phalsipherum.

Phalsipherum is a fatal disease caused by a rare kind of mosquito. This insect is larger than normal mosquitoes and can only fly upto a foot high. It is found only in Goa.

When Perulekar woke up, he was not able to breathe properly, and his health started deteriorating with each passing day. One evening, when he woke up, he found Konkar by his side. He was happy to see him. He wanted to warn Konkar and tell him what he had learned, but he was not able to speak properly. He was not able to explain anything. His condition was not stable. Konkar tried very hard to understand his actions but to no avail. The doctor asked him to leave the patient alone.

That night, Perulekar's breathing grew faster and suddenly stopped. He was no more. He had tried very hard to help his friend, even in his last moments, but things didn't turn out as he had thought they would.

With the keys in their possession, along with the receipt-agreement of ownership of the hotel, Malini and Neeraj went to Punjab to bring the sixty-one aspirants to Goa, after selling them the dream of working in Dubai. The labourers were asked to work hard. They were not allowed to venture too far from the hotel premises, with the excuse of not having a valid visa to visit the city. The workers had no idea that they were being fooled or that there was no such thing as a 'city visiting visa'. The poor labourers, who had been brought to Goa instead of

Fujairah, were too naïve to realize that they had been cheated by these fraudsters. Not until Ajit Pal Singh revealed the truth to them.

∽

Ajit Pal was furious when he came to know what had transpired and how the sophisticated, soft-spoken couple had befooled all of them. He informed his co-workers about how the placement agency had duped them. The sixty-one men from Punjab were now frantic. Together, they beat up the security guards and then marched to the nearby Porvorim police station to lodge a complaint, but the police were of little help. Apart from noting down the complaint of the workers, they could do nothing, because the labourers had no documents to support their case. Their passports were with the agency. The police said they would investigate the matter and sent them back to the hotel.

The poor men were helpless. The police never turned up, nor did Neeraj. Their only hope was Pran Kohli who told them he had no idea what was going on. They would have to wait for the proprietor to come, he said, who was travelling and would return in a few days. The men waited, sitting idle, refusing to pick up their tools without first having a word with the agency. The Arab employer, who was always spotted in his traditional Arabian attire, was nowhere to be seen.

Three days before Ajit Pal's discovery, Neeraj had met Konkar and told him that Malini had suddenly fallen ill. The doctors suspected the development of malignancy in her abdomen. There was a chance of her going in for surgery at the Tata Cancer Hospital in Mumbai. The cheque worth ₹2 crores that they had handed over the last time had bounced, and Neeraj apologized for the same, handing over another post-dated cheque to Konkar.

This too was signed by Malini.

Dilip Konkar complained about the large workforce that had been staying at his hotel, but Neeraj gave him a reassuring pat, saying, 'Give me just ten days.' He explained that his wife—who was the boss, after all—would then be in a position to return to Goa. Neeraj promised he would clear all outstanding payments in one go. Konkar, though utterly confused, was pleased to know that Malini was the boss and not Neeraj. He compared himself with Neeraj, who was much more handsome, but convinced himself to be one up on him in personality.

Konkar was upset after hearing about the ill-health of someone he had come to desire and believe in. He wished he could meet Malini immediately. Looking at Neeraj, he softened up, finding it difficult to press his charges too forcefully. Neeraj took out two diamond-studded gold necklaces and gave them to Konkar. 'They were priceless and belonged to the royal family of Punjab,' he said. Konkar relented. He agreed to give them ten days to clear all the payments that included the balance consideration of ₹1.50 crores.

Neeraj left for Mumbai in his Mercedes. That was the last time Konkar ever saw Neeraj or Malini. Neither did Malini have cancer, nor was she hospitalized. She was in Mumbai's famous jewellery market purchasing gold biscuits and ornaments from every reputed jeweller, with the cash they had taken from the poor labourers of Punjab and from James D'Souza. Neeraj met her in Mumbai and after taking a portion of the jewellery and some money, he left for Manali, where he took up work at a restaurant and started leading an obscure life. As for Malini, no one ever saw her again. It was as if she just vanished into thin air.

Before the stipulated ten days were over, when there was no

sign of Neeraj or Malini, Konkar lost patience. Along with some of his staff, he went to his hotel and yelled at the labourers, now holding possession of the premises. He ordered them to vacate his hotel immediately. It had been a few days since the workers had been sitting idle, waiting. They were a tired, angry and impatient lot, and they refused to budge from there. Ajit Pal told Konkar of the fraud carried out on them and how they were duped by the placement agency. He was adamant that they would not leave until their money was returned to them and arrangements were made to send them back to Punjab. 'We also want compensation,' he said. A heated argument ensued between the two factions. One of the guards summoned the police and only then, things were brought under control. The police noted the complaints on either side. Word of the fight had already spread. Konkar's arch business rival, James D'Souza, with two of his lawyers, arrived at the hotel and intervened in the melee.

He showed the police two agreements, in the original. One was executed for ₹4 crores by Dilip Konkar in favour of Neeraj and Malini, and the second agreement indicated that the latter had further sold their rights of the hotel to James D'Souza for ₹4.50 crores. James D'Souza claimed that Malini had given him the possession of the hotel and nobody could dispossess him of his property. He had all the signed documents with him. According to him, Malini had promised to register the 'Agreement to Sell' document on her next visit to Goa, but had suddenly fallen ill. It was also a fact that James D'Souza had agreed to proceed with this arrangement, since it was not mandatory to register the 'agreement to sell' during those days.

Dilip Konkar snatched the two agreements and went through them. He was shocked to see the clause in the agreement signed by him that stated the handing over of the possession of the hotel to Malini on receipt of ₹50 lakhs. He wondered how he could have been so naïve to give away the possession, on receiving one-eighth of the agreed price.

Both, Konkar and D'Souza, were compelled to lodge their respective complaints along with a detailed description of the two miscreants. A case was registered with the Goa Police in Porvorim, under Section 420 of the Indian Penal Code. Due to the complex nature of the case, it was later transferred to the police headquarters in Panjim.

Inspector Tambe was assigned the case by Deputy General of Police, H.S. Brar. The former began to collect evidence and recorded the statements of the poor labourers. He then left for Punjab. The Punjab police, by now, had received complaints from various people, including three employees of a Ludhiana office and its landlord, Sardar Santokh Singh. The landlord told the inspector that he had not been paid rent for the past three months. The staff informed that they had not received their salary and that their employer had suddenly disappeared. The complaints continued to pour in against the absconding couple for non-payment of dues, with a long list of frauds committed, but there was no sign of the duo. The enormity of the fraud made this a big sensation, with the story being covered by all major newspapers.

Inspector Tambe returned to Goa and reported his findings to his superiors. He revealed what had transpired in Goa and Punjab and disclosed the details of the fraud committed by Neeraj and Malini—of how they had duped the poor and innocent labourers to the tune of ₹3 crores. The police had a photograph of the couple that Konkar had taken during the first party the latter attended. This was printed in the newspapers in Goa. The police announced a reward for any concrete information that anyone could give regarding the so-called 'royal couple'.

The police organized a search party to track down Neeraj and Malini. The two were neither in any police records nor in any government records. None of them had been issued a passport or owned any immovable property. Inspector Tambe drew a blank as far as the identity of the couple was concerned. Nobody—neither the labourers, nor Konkar and D'Souza—had checked the antecedents of the couple. All of them—including Santokh Singh and Pran Kohli—had believed the couples' story regarding their ancestors being a part of the royal family of one of the princely estates of Punjab.

Inspector Tambe returned to Punjab once again, this time to the office of Star Placement Agency in Ludhiana. He confiscated their books, records and documents. He looked for the couple's bank records, but could find nothing. In a table drawer, under some files, there lay a single chequebook with the joint names of Subhash Talwar and Ramesh Talwar printed on it.

In the absence of any other clue, the inspector followed this one lead. And to his surprise, this lead paid off when he arrived at the bank to which the chequebook belonged. The manager cooperated with the investigation and shared with the inspector the account opening documents related to the account number, including the photographs of the Talwars. The inspector compared the pictures to the ones he had of the couple, and he immediately recognized Neeraj, who had given his name as Subhash Talwar. He did not know the other person in the photograph. And where was Malini?

The inspector returned to Goa and once again, questioned Konkar about the people who had introduced him to the couple. Konkar gave the names of two property brokers in the Calangute area. On questioning them, it was learned that a couple who showed interest in both purchasing a hotel as well as renting accommodation had approached the brokers. Luckily, Pran Kohli happened to be present at one of the broker's office at that time. He wished to rent his own accommodation, so he immediately struck a deal with the couple.

The police asked the sub-inspector to make inquiries about Pran Kohli, who was not originally from Goa. Their suspicions came true. The sub-inspector had startling revelations to share. Pran Kohli's real name was Satinder Bir, and he was from Rohtak. He used to run a chit fund company. He was the son of a police constable posted at Rohtak Police Station in Haryana. When his company went bankrupt, he owed almost ₹50 lakhs to the investors. He, along with his two accomplices—Rampal Singh and Lakhanpal Singh—had then absconded from Rohtak. The whereabouts of the three men were unknown. After two years and a manhunt that reached nowhere, the police had declared the three as fugitives and registered a case against them. With no success and no further clues, the files were consigned to the records as non-existent.

Further inquiries about Satinder Bir, masquerading as Pran Kohli, revealed that there were more than ten cases of fraud, smuggling, theft and extortion, pending in various courts in Haryana, against him. He was proclaimed an offender and absconder. No one in Rohtak who knew Satinder Bir, had any idea that he lived in Goa under the guise of Pran Kohli.

Inspector Tambe visited Rohtak to confirm the report he had been given by his sub-inspector. The police records confirmed everything he had heard. Indeed, Pran Kohli was Satinder Bir, and he had two accomplices Rampal and Lakhanpal. Neeraj Singh, alias Subhash Talwar, was, in fact, Rampal Singh. And, Ramesh

Talwar and Lakhanpal were the same people. The inspector also found out that Rampal Singh was a bachelor. Both he and his brother Lakhanpal were described to be over-ambitious, and they had spent more money than they had ever earned on liquor and gambling. The two brothers were tricksters. Tall and good-looking, they could easily convince anyone to invest money with them. Their chit-fund business had failed miserably due to their reckless spending. They had closed down their business offices overnight and absconded from Rohtak about three years ago. No one in the city had ever seen them after that.

The inspector made discreet inquiries in Ludhiana and questioned the staff of Star Placement Agency. It was revealed that Neeraj and Malini had opened the plush offices some four months back, and had given advertisements for aspirants required for jobs in the UAE and Canada. Many people had shown interest, including some educated and skilled workers. Neeraj had instructed the staff at his office to entertain only uneducated applicants. Neeraj and Malini had hired a huge house in Civil Lines, Ludhiana, thrown parties, inviting their landlord, Santokh Singh, and other elite people and offered them precious gifts. After gaining their confidence, the duo had selected sixty-one men, mostly young and uneducated, to offer them jobs in the UAE on a letterhead of a hotel in Fujairah. They had collected three crores from these innocent youth for providing jobs in UAE. The sole purpose of the duo was to swindle as much money from the unemployed youth in Punjab in lieu of jobs offered at the UAE.

The inspector returned to Goa and arrested Pran Kohli. On questioning the latter, he told the police the truth. 'Neeraj approached me through a friend to help him in the purchase of a hotel in Goa, but I have no knowledge of the placement agency or any other businesses of Neeraj,' he admitted.

Inspector Tambe had taken the case up as a challenge. He simply had to solve this intriguing mystery. One evening, he was watching a movie. One of the scenes showed two male actors masquerading as females. That was when the idea struck him! He wondered aloud, 'Malini, for all we know, may not be Malini at all. Of course! Otherwise, how could she disappear into thin air?' And he began working on that theory.

The photographs of Lakhanpal, alias Ramesh Talwar, that he had gotten from Ludhiana and Rohtak, could not establish the truth. So, the inspector went all the way to Rampal Singh's parents in Ludhiana. There, he had an entire album to support his case. The pictures confirmed it all. The photographs of Lakhanpal Singh were compared with that of Malini's. The height and features were identical, and with make-up on his face, Lakhanpal could easily masquerade as Malini. The discovery shook Inspector Tambe, and he immediately passed on this vital information to his superiors in Goa.

Dilip Konkar and James D'Souza were shown the photographs. They accepted, extremely sheepishly, that Lakhanpal Singh resembled Malini. The two were shocked, 'How could they have fallen for her charms? For a man seducing them?'

'If Malini was not a female and was only disguised as Neeraj's wife, what could the reason have been?' Konkar was intrigued and exceedingly annoyed with himself.

The inspector smiled mockingly and replied, 'They wanted to take advantage of the inherent weakness of men. There are many who are gullible towards good-looking women, especially if a woman allows them a little leeway.'

Konkar and D'Souza could not sleep that night. They could not digest the fact that they had been taken for a ride by a woman. What would their wives say when they heard about it? The very thought of Malini infuriated them now. However, they had no choice but to blame themselves.

After two months, the police finally caught up with Lakhanpal in Oshiwara in Bombay. He was working as a salesman under the name of Ramesh Talwar from Ludhiana. He was brought to Goa and interrogated. He confessed that he and his brother had masqueraded as the couple and that it was Rampal's idea that Lakhanpal acted as his wife. He also disclosed the whereabouts of Rampal's alias, Neeraj. A police team was rushed to the restaurant in Manali where they found the fraudster working under a different guise. He was arrested by the sub-inspector with the help of the Manali police.

The money that they had looted was recovered from various private lockers. Ajit Pal and the other labourers—the poor victims of the clever fraud—were paid back on a pro-rata basis, and their return to Punjab was arranged. As for Dilip Konkar and James D'Souza, the Income Tax Department took appropriate action against them for accepting and paying so much cash for the hotel transaction. Poor Konkar, he had received one shock after another. The final one was that all the jewellery and other gifts that Neeraj and Malini had given to him turned out to be fake. They were replicas of original jewellery. The Rolex was also a fake, easily available in Ulhaas Nagar near Mumbai for just ₹500.

Rampal and Lakhanpal were sentenced to prison by the Punjab and Haryana Court for fourteen years under several sections of the Indian Penal Code. They were lodged in Rohtak Jail and did not contest the verdict when they learned that several farmers and labourers from Punjab had vowed to beat them up once they were released from prison. Rampal and Lakhanpal felt safer behind bars and requested the courts to shift them to Tihar Jail in Delhi, fearing for their lives.

The fraud committed by them became sensational news. The newspapers and TV titled the headline as 'Masqueraders from the North'.

Rickshaw Faridabadi

The romantic story of a rich girl falling in love with a rickshaw puller, having a narrative for the years gone by is heartbreaking, to say the least. The idea of the story was provided by Dr Ravi Gulati of Norway and producer of the film Desert Tears.

This story is replete with love, emotions, poverty and interpersonal relationships. It has been assigned to a film production company known as The Northern Lights owned by Dr Ravi Gulati and Mr Himanshu Gulati, deputy minister of justice in Oslo, Norway. Their latest movie, Desert Tears *has made waves in the film fraternity for being one of the best art films screened in recent times.*

The producers and directors intend to film the scenes in Faridabad and Norway, especially trying to capture the picturesque Northern Lights.

A black luxury sedan left a palatial house situated in the posh Sector 15 of Faridabad—an industrial town adjacent to New Delhi. Reema Khanna was the owner of this extravagantly built house, constructed on the lines of ancient Greek architecture. The property covered a built-up area of 2,000 square yards and comprised ten bedrooms, an enormous well-decorated living room, two elevators, a terrace garden and a swimming pool.

Reema was in a hurry to attend a meeting at Hotel Taj Vivanta in Surajkund, about 13 km from home. Her driver had not turned up. The meeting was scheduled for 6 p.m., and it was already close to 7, and frantic calls from her real estate agent had made her press the panic button.

Reema and her Norwegian doctor husband Ravi Khanna were looking to set up a chain of hospitals in tier-2 cities. The idea was to purchase old, ill-equipped hospitals in India and convert them into modern ones, offering the best medical care. This was the first meeting she was to have with the owners of the well-known hospital chain, Jeev-Daya Hospitals. The meeting was an important one because the Jeev-Daya Group had hospitals in several tier-2 cities in India. Buying over the group meant hitting, not two, but many birds with one stone. With the signing of a single contract, the rich Khannas of Norway could own a number of established hospitals in various cities. Dr Ravi Khanna had another reason for buying hospitals. It was an emotional decision to do so. Sometime back, he had received a call from his brother who lived in Faridabad. The latter had informed him about the untimely demise of four of his acquaintances. Six members of his friend's family, travelling on a highway, had met with an accident and had been severely injured. There were only two available oxygen cylinders at the hospital they had been admitted to. Consequently, only two of the six injured could be saved. Four lives were lost due to the lack of basic emergency equipment.

It was finally time to serve their country of birth. The couple had decided that Reema would initiate negotiations with the hospitals they had shortlisted in India, and Ravi would join her in two weeks.

Reema drove out of her sector, turned left onto the main highway and accelerated the luxury car. 'Faridabad has changed so much. It used to be a dusty industrial town, and now it is becoming a modern commercial city,' she said to herself. 'Metro trains and air-conditioned malls have changed the geography of Faridabad. And flyovers have made movement quicker and easier,' she observed. In spite of being in a hurry, she could not help but notice the changes she saw every time she was on the road. 'Oh, Faridabad! I do miss your old-world charm!'

She was in Faridabad after a gap of almost thirty years. The pollution levels had not lowered, but the infrastructural development matched any flourishing city in a developing economy. The latest models of cars buzzed passed her, and she remembered that the Prime Minister himself had selected Faridabad to be developed as a "smart city". Henna alone was bringing in crores of rupees through export to Faridabad. 'No doubt it is a progressive city,' and she nodded her head in affirmation, taking a U-turn from Bata Chowk.

She was plying at a very high speed as she took the Neelam Flyover at Ajronda Chowk. The metro station that ran alongside buzzed with activity. The metro had suddenly become the most sought-after means of transport in the National Capital Region, especially on account of Faridabad's close proximity to Central Delhi. It was a dark winter evening, and the traffic was at its peak. Reema descended the flyover at the same speed without realizing that a lot of people leaving the metro station took rickshaws from that point, to reach their respective homes.

Suddenly, from a narrow side lane next to a petrol station, an old man riding a rickshaw exited on to the main road right in front of her. Reema slammed on the brakes, but it was too late. The impact was tremendous. Her Mercedes S-500 rammed into him in full force, throwing him up in the air. The man took a few summersaults before falling on the road with a dull thud.

The rickshaw puller lay sprawled, face downwards, critically injured and bleeding profusely. He was a frail, skinny, white-haired man. His old and dilapidated rickshaw lay against the pavement in pieces. Suddenly, the gravity of the situation dawned on Reema. Speeding on a highway amidst mixed traffic during rush hour was indeed asking for big trouble.

'I should not have been on the wheels,' she said, cursing herself. She may have been born and brought up in Faridabad, but she had forgotten how unpredictable the traffic could be. Driving a Mercedes in Oslo was different from driving the same vehicle in a crowded industrial town.

People rushed to the spot. The unconscious man needed immediate medical attention. Reema got out of her car. She looked elegant in her expensive silk saree and glittering emerald necklace and hardly looked like an Indian after having spent so many years in Europe. Any other instance following such an incident, and the local people, especially the rickshaw pullers, would have beaten the driver up. But in this instance, no one dared touch this rich woman who commanded their respect. Yes, the people were angry, and Reema found herself profusely apologizing, admitting to her mistake.

Somebody had called the police, and soon, two police vans appeared. Sub-inspector Hukum Singh took control of the situation. The rickshaw puller was taken to the nearest hospital, Jeev-Daya.

Hukum Singh instructed Reema to leave the car and accompany him, first to the hospital, and then to the police station, where her statement would be recorded under Section 164 of the IPC Act. However, Reema refused, saying that she would like to call her friend first and only then accompany him.

Reema's mobile phone and her expensive Louis Vuitton bag containing a lot of money were in the car. But, in the ensuing confusion, she had left the vehicle unlocked. To her dismay, she found both items missing. Taking advantage of all the commotion, someone had stolen them. She called off her meeting after borrowing the sub-inspector's phone, and then she called her close friend Roshni, who lived in Sector 10. The latter arrived in a few minutes, and Reema was able to use her phone to call her husband in Oslo. She apprised him of the accident. Then, the two women, along with the police personnel, headed for the hospital.

It was 9.30 p.m. when a team of lawyers appeared at the emergency ward of the hospital. Dr Ravi Khanna had warned his wife not to speak to anyone, especially the police. She was instructed to wait until his lawyers arrived. Now the team of lawyers arrived, armed with a story to save her—that her driver Ram Singh had been driving the car. She was not the one at the wheel when the poor rickshaw puller was hit.

Reema protested vehemently and told the lawyers that she could not possibly do that. There were many witnesses at the scene of the incident, and she would not allow the driver to be punished for her reckless act. She narrated the details of the ghastly event to them, but the lawyers advised not to confess or sign any statement.

The lawyers assured her that Ram Singh had agreed to take responsibility. He was ready to confess—be it for causing severe injuries, or even to face a more serious sentence in case the injured man succumbed to his injuries. It was serious business, and the lawyers were able to convince her not to take the blame. Reema understood and heeded their suggestion. Her husband was an important client of the lawyers, and so, they acted swiftly, with an intention to take her away from the inquisitive eyes of Hukum Singh.

The police recorded driver Ram Singh's statement. He had appeared miraculously, taking all responsibility for the accident. At first, they were not convinced at the sudden emergence of the driver, and interrogated him thoroughly. They were unwilling to accommodate this new turn of events. The lawyers, however, pressed on with their case, and with some persuasion, they were able to get the sub-inspector to lend an ear to Ram Singh's version.

In the meantime, the rickshaw puller was rushed to the operation theatre where the surgeons tried to save him as best as they could, given the medical equipment they had. His condition, however, deteriorated and he drifted into a coma. This further allowed the lawyers to successfully plant their story, and Reema was free to go. As she descended the stairs leading to the reception area of the hospital, still reeling under the course of events, she saw an exact lookalike of Raj Kumar Sehrawat, alias Raju, rushing in. She stood transfixed.

Raju, her closest college mate, her first love, was right in front of her eyes. It took her a few seconds to realize that Raju would have also grown old by now, and this young lookalike could not be her old classmate. This had to be someone else.

She felt like she had gone back some thirty-five years, to a time when she had befriended Raju. They went everywhere together, from tuitions to college. They were in love with each other. With one more look at the young lad, who was now standing at the reception with a worried expression, she concluded that he had to be Raju's bloodline. She was intrigued. 'Would she be able to meet Raju through his son?'

Her heart beat faster. Her lawyers were astonished to see her standing as though immobilized. They wanted to take her away from any further police interrogation. But Reema was not going anywhere until she had uncovered the mystery of this chance encounter.

The youngster was enquiring about an accident case that had occurred at Neelam Chowk. 'The injured had been brought to the emergency ward,' she overheard him say. It suddenly dawned on her that the person she had hit had been Raju himself!

She walked towards the young lad, all the while trying to keep her emotions in check. Placing a hand on his shoulder, she asked, 'Are you Raj Kumar's son? I almost mistook you for him.' She spoke with a lump in her throat.

'Yes, I am. Do you know my father? Is he alright? Is he badly hurt? Why don't these people provide information about him? Who are you, and how do you know my father? How did you know I am his son?' He threw a barrage of questions at her, anxious as he was about his father's condition.

Now he turned and yelled at the receptionist, 'Why are you not telling me how my father is? Who was responsible for the accident? Who was driving the car? Why don't you answer my questions?'

Tears trickled down Reema's cheeks. Raju's son understood that something untoward had occurred. He had no idea who this woman was, but he was sure that something terrible had befallen his father.

When he was finally informed where his father was, the boy, whose name was Rahul, ran up to the first floor where the operation theatre was. The area was abuzz with activity. Nurses ran in and out of the operation theatre with blood packs and medicines. The surgeons were putting in their best efforts. They had received strict instructions from the managing director of the hospital to try everything possible to save the life of the rickshaw puller. Two lateral ribs had protruded into his lungs and caused an irreparable injury. A lot of blood had been lost, and his heartbeat plummeted. They could barely manage to keep his vital signs under control. Rahul was anxious and wanted to meet the surgeons, but he was asked to wait for the doctors to come out of the operation theatre.

'How could I be so reckless?' Reema asked herself again and again. 'How could I injure the very person that I once loved from the core of my heart?'

∽

He was an outstanding sportsman and good at studies as well. He had always helped her solve complex accountancy and mathematical problems in college. He was the one who had supported her in all her endeavours during their wonderful college days more than three decades back.

Reema, waiting outside the operation theatre late that night, walked down the memory lane. Years back, when she was merely nineteen years old, she had met Raju for the first time. He was an attentive student with good looks, an above-average height, wheatish complexion and a sharp nose. His curly hair and the cleft on his chin made girls go gaga over him.

He came from a financially poor background and had been reprimanded by the principal for not being able to pay the college fees on time. In spite of that he was smart, knowledgeable and bright. He was confident about himself. Reema had only exchanged pleasantries with Raj Kumar Sehrawat, never spoken to him at length, but she found him to be a combination of genuine humility and goodness. He had a fan following among the girls, but she had never shown any interest in him.

When she was in Fatima Convent School in Sector 14, her orthodox father made sure that she did not go out of her house alone. But her brother, who was two years younger than her, had the liberty to roam around anywhere he wanted. Now that she was in college, she was allowed a little freedom. Reema's parents allowed her to go to the market and for her Math's tuition, all by herself. They decided that she no longer needed a chaperone to escort her to nearby places during the daytime. At times, her brother drove her in their car to her Math tutor's house in an adjacent sector, a kilometre and a half away from her home, while on other days she went by rickshaw. Occasionally, her close friend, Roshni Siddiqui, accompanied her on these visits.

Reema was regular with her tuitions. On one such rickshaw trip, when she held out a two-rupee note to pay the rickshaw puller, he seemed to behave a little strange. He seemed to hesitate while taking the money. He had his face covered with a black and white striped cotton scarf, so she was not able to see his expression. She thought that maybe he wanted more money but brushed it aside.

A few days later, she noticed that she had hired the same rickshaw puller. He had his face covered with the same black and white scarf as earlier. He dropped her off at the lecturer's house, and waited outside her tutor's house when she finished her class, which seemed rather strange. It began to happen often. She simply assumed that he hung around since she was an assured passenger. She had never seen his face; he kept it covered just like many other rickshaw pullers.

On a particularly windy day, the rickshaw puller's scarf blew away, and Reema could not believe her eyes. She recognized Raju, her classmate from college. She had heard that in spite of belonging to a good family, he was on hard times. Raju was embarrassed, but he recovered from that awkward moment and requested her not to reveal his identity and ordeal to other classmates, or they would make fun of him.

He sheepishly explained to her that after college hours, he rode his rickshaw to earn extra money for survival. Many in college knew that after his father's death in an accident, his family had fallen on difficult days. His father had been a salesman in a private company, and they had lived a reasonably good life, but after his father's demise, circumstances had changed drastically. From being a middle-class family, they had now become poor. Their standard of living and lifestyle changed to the current situation, where it was difficult for them to have two meals a day.

The compensation, provident fund and gratuity money received from the private company were utilized when his two elder sisters were married to two brothers in Mathura. He lived with his mother and gradually, all their funds depleted. The mother and son now lived in one room of their house in Ballabgarh, and they had sublet the other two rooms. Reema listened to him intently. He dropped her at the lecturer's house and assured her that he would return after an hour to take her back to her residence. She offered him a two-rupee note, which this time he politely refused. After an hour, she found him waiting for her, and he dropped her home.

That routine continued for some time. He would take her to her tutor's residence and then wait outside or return to take her back home. He explained to her that although he lived in Ballabgarh, he plied his rickshaw in these sectors, some kilometres away from his home, so as to not reveal that fact to his neighbours. He once again requested her to keep this facet of his life to herself, and she assured him of her silence, becoming his confidante of sorts.

One night, Reema could not sleep, and she kept thinking about Raju. She had never touched a man's hand so firmly until that evening when on the way back, he had held her hand. Although his intention had been only to support her as she alighted from his rickshaw, the touch had triggered some emotions. After all, the need to feel loved is a primary human emotion, and Reema and Raju were only human. She had, many a time, noticed admiration in his eyes, but had, so far, avoided making eye contact with him. She did not dare look back. As she continued to think of that evening, there was a sudden rush of blood and an urge to have that physical contact with Raju again.

The more she thought about him, the more her attraction towards Raju increased. She knew the humongous difference between her status and his miserable condition. She kept questioning herself, 'Are you really in love with this guy?' Despite answering in the negative, her mind drifted to romantic thoughts about him.

She dreamed of distant mountains, a rainbow shining bright. And while crossing a river with crystal-clear water, she spotted Raju standing on the bank of the river with open arms. She drew closer to him, and he promised to cross the oceans, traverse desert sands and endure all untold hardships for her. She woke up with a jolt, and to her relief, realized that it was only a dream.

She brushed aside the sweet dream knowing completely well that such expressions of thoughts and feelings were not encouraged by the elders in her family. Rather, they would strongly condemn them.

Sunil Kapoor, in conversation with Field Marshal Arjun Singh, during the book launch of The Peacock Feather *at United Service Institution Residency.*

Presenting the book The Peacock Feather *to Prime Minister Narendra Modi.*

Sunil Kapoor with veteran actor Dharmendra.

Sunil Kapoor donning the hat of an actor for the movie Tiger Trail.

Receiving the blessings from former Prime Minister Dr Manmohan Singh.

Sunil Kapoor presenting the book, The Peacock Feather, *to the late senior politician Arun Jaitley.*

Veteran actor Jeetendra launching the book, The Peacock Feather *and its CD.*

Identical twins, Sunil Kapoor and Sudhir Kapoor, posing with Neelam Mukherjee, wife of the late Joy Mukherjee.

Sunil Kapoor with producer and director Abbas Mastan during a prolonged discussion.

Sunil Kapoor presenting the book The Peacock Feather *to Congress leader Oscar Fernandes.*

Author Sunil Kapoor descending the stairs of the Supreme Court in New Delhi.

Sunil Kapoor with Manoj Tiwari at the CD launch of Punam ka Chaand.

Author Sunil Kapoor with Senior Politician Amar Singh.

Sunil Kapoor in conversation with music maestro Anandji Virji Shah.

Authors Sunil Kapoor and Sudhir Kapoor holding the coveted Dadasaheb Phalke Award for the film Ab Mujhe Udna Hai, *based on the short story 'Let Me Soar High' in* A Ticklish Affair and Other Short Stories, *in 2019.*

Sunil Kapoor and Sudhir Kapoor during the launch of the book, The Peacock Feather, *by Mohammad Rafi's son, Shahid Rafi.*

The next day in college was not the same as the days gone by. Time and again, Reema and Raju exchanged glances. She was mature enough to understand that furrowed brows, trembling hands and eye movements gave a certain clue as to what a person was feeling. She could not speak to him in private in college. Rumours would spread like wildfire. Any action from either side could land her in trouble.

That same evening, Reema took special care to dress well for her tuition. She even wore some perfume for the first time. En route, the unpredictable weather paved the way for a romantic occurrence. Just as they were nearing a temple, it first started to drizzle, and then quickly turned into a downpour. Both alighted from the rickshaw and ran for shelter under a banyan tree. For some inexplicable reason, or maybe, a natural urge, she drew very close to Raju. Instinctively, he put his arm around her. The closeness sparked something and she felt blood rush through her veins.

She turned towards him and looked at his face. He read the message. She was longing for him. He bent a little and kissed her on her lips. It was, as though, lightning had passed through her trembling body. The pleasure she felt was immense. He looked into her eyes and said shyly, 'I love you,' and then, he kissed her again. The rain lightened, but being completely drenched, she asked to be dropped back home.

The next evening turned out to be even more exciting than the one before. On the way to her tuition, she asked him to turn the rickshaw towards Neelam Theatre, a short distance away. She wanted to watch the Dharmendra and Amitabh Bachchan starrer, *Sholay*, even if it meant she could watch the movie only for the duration of her tuition timings. The film had been running for several months at the same theatre, and she had seen it before.

The picture was such that it could be seen innumerable times.

The thrill of bunking her tuition and watching a movie was unmatched. She had always wanted to do something like this. She bought the tickets and a single coke and popcorn. While sitting next to each other, she took his arm and placed it across her shoulders. She had purposely bought the expensive box seats.

'You are giving me ideas,' he said naughtily.

She smiled mischievously and replied, 'You boys will never understand a girl's feelings.' Reaching out, she messed his hair playfully.

'That's not true. I love you and can't imagine doing anything without your consent. I would do nothing to hurt your feelings.'

He bent forward and kissed her. This time, sitting in the box, devoid of any other cinema-goer, she drew closer to him and allowed him to kiss her for a long time.

He smiled and said, 'I really care for you. Can I call you Princess instead of Reema? You are no less than a princess for this "Faridabadi rickshaw puller".'

She laughed at the word "Faridabadi". 'What is this Faridabadi business?' she chided him.

'Well, a commoner in Faridabad is a Faridabadi, and a princess like you, granddaughter of Rai Bahadur Mulk Raj Sethi—the owner of Cooline Gears—is a different breed altogether. You live in bungalows, and we live in small houses. Your grandfather still carries a gold pocket watch, with a gold chain, and changes his attire before dining, whereas we have our food sitting on wooden planks in the kitchen.'

'You seem to know a lot about us,' she retorted.

'Reema, I am a rickshaw puller, a small-time man. I have seen really bad days after my father died.' He said, 'The euphoria of "being in love" will always give us the illusion that we have an intimate relationship. We will have strong feelings towards each other. Our obsession and our longing for each other will create a false sense that we are made for each other.' His words of wisdom had her look at him in bewilderment. 'We fail to reconcile with the reality of human nature. By nature, we are all egocentric. Our world revolves around us alone. This infatuation, this euphoria, gives us that illusion.'

'That's absurd! You and your baseless philosophy are preposterous, Raju. I am truly in love with you. For some time now, I have not been able to do anything properly. I keep thinking about you, and my world now revolves around you. Believe me, I don't even feel the presence of my family in my house, or for that matter, my friends in college. I just want to be with you, you and only you. No one else. I wish I could be with you forever,' she spoke, in one breath.

'Love is a choice and cannot be forced.' Raju was more sober than ever. 'Look Reema, our status are poles apart...' but before he could go any further, she put a finger on his lips. 'Can we skip all this stupid talk? Shouldn't we enjoy being together in this darkness? After all, we are in love, you silly Faridabadi.'

Raju started to say something, but she clasped his hand and said, 'Shut up, you Rickshaw Faridabadi and just look into my eyes.' He smiled.

'Oh god, Reema! Your eyes are so beautiful. I could drown in them. I am sure I will die in your arms one day, and you alone will be responsible for my death,' he laughed and continued, 'but if I die in your arms, I would do so happily.'

She got up from her seat. 'Look, Raju, time is ticking. Any further delay and my father will be worried. Drop me home quickly.' She spoke with urgency. Reluctantly, Raju got up and left the movie hall with her.

On the way out, he asked her about her mother. Reema's vivacious mood changed into a sober one. She told him her mother had died when she was five years old.

The next day, Reema asked Raju, 'So how did you like the movie, Rickshaw Faridabadi?'

'What movie are you talking about? I was only looking at your beautiful face,' he retorted. 'You are more beautiful than Hema Malini. You are the most beautiful girl on earth!'

She gave him a questioning look. 'Do you mean that?'

'Cross my heart,' he said. He continued, smiling, 'You called me "Faridabadi" madam. Do you know that Faridabad was established on the banks of River Yamuna, close to the Delhi Sultanate in the seventeenth century, by Emperor Jahangir in the memory of the respected and revered Sufi Saint, Farid? The emperor had tremendous respect and faith in the saint. The people of Faridabad are blessed by Saint Farid, and that's why we have lived here happily even if with meagre means.' Reema was impressed by his knowledge about the city she was born in.

This routine of bunking tuitions to meet each other continued, and they grew closer to each other. One day, he took her to his house to meet his ailing mother, Sita Devi. The timing was bad. His mother, though unwell, was being yelled at by a neighbour for not having stitched a salwar-suit correctly. In spite of the embarrassment, Sita Devi went out of her way to be hospitable to Reema, who developed an immense liking for the love and affection displayed by the mother. She was a simple and devoted woman, and to Reema, it was a pleasure being with her. Sita Devi took a liking to Reema too, but later she cautioned her son regarding the difference in status between the two families.

There were days when Reema had to walk to her tutor's

home or hire another rickshaw, because Raju was occupied with looking after his ailing mother. At times, he would get busy with meeting the unending demands of his two brothers-in-law. He had to visit them regularly to carry out their wishes. Festivals, especially, were a curse for him as then; he had to, perforce, buy sweetmeat boxes and fruit baskets as gifts to be given to the in-laws. This was particularly difficult for Raju who was in debt and unable to pay the interest amount to a moneylender, Janki Dass, who was his landlord. The latter was a shrewd businessman and would adopt any means to recover his money.

In Raju's absence, life for Reema moved very slowly. She did not like the arrogant attitude of his brothers-in-law and felt sorry for him. Once, while taking her for her class, he showed her the newly painted letters at the back of his rickshaw: 'Rickshaw Faridabadi'. Both laughed at the coined phrase, and it amused her greatly that he had painted the label she had given him.

The last time she saw Raju was when he was plying his rickshaw near Neelam Chowk. She was with her father in their car. Raju did not see her then.

Her romance came to an abrupt end when Raju stopped attending college. Reema came to know from a classmate that he had injured his landlord seriously after the latter tried to forcibly evict Raju and his mother from their house for not paying his dues, and for subletting the rooms. He was arrested and sent behind bars. Raju's name was struck off college rolls. Neither did Reema have any further information about what really happened, nor could she talk to anybody about it. She made several trips to his house but found the doors locked.

'Mrs Khanna?' A voice similar to that of Raju's brought her back to the present. Rahul stood in front of her with tears in his eyes. He blamed her driver for his father's untimely death. 'He was only fifty-four years old. What harm had he ever done to you? You rich people who travel in big cars do not care what happens to us poor people. The police have told me that according to your lawyers you are willing to give compensation for my father's death. Can you bring my poor father back to life?' A relative took him aside while he wept bitterly. Reema could not believe what she had just heard. Raju was dead! Her Raju was no more, and she was the reason for it.

She stood outside the operation theatre, not knowing how to react. She had killed her first love. She had killed the man who had embraced her and kissed her for the first time when she was only nineteen. Who knew the girl sitting next to him in the theatre years back would be the one who would take his life. He had often teased her that instead of living apart, he would rather die in her arms. The words, 'One day I will die in your arms,' came back to her. Yes, that was what he had said, and that was what was destined.

She walked towards Rahul, who was weeping hysterically. She tried to console him, but he would not let her. He said bitterly, 'I am the only child of my parents. My mother has just died of asthma. Hardly two months have passed, and you have made me an orphan. Why on earth was I born to bear such tragedy? Could you please ask your driver to run over me too?' He was angry, distraught and went berserk. It was natural for him to react in that manner, she thought and looked sympathetically at him, but he turned away as if to dismiss her presence.

Reema had no idea how to handle the situation. Her thoughts were with Raju, who had lived in poverty for most of his life.

She felt guilty because she had led a luxurious life in Norway and other European countries. She remembered that while Raju had served his sentence in prison, she had compromised with her prevailing circumstances and with great difficulty, agreed for her marriage. She had then left for Oslo to start a new life with Dr Ravi Khanna. Later, she had done a course in physiotherapy to become one of the best therapists in Oslo. She had taken over the management of her husband's hospital and excelled at it.

She remembered that due to the paucity of funds and being booked for criminal acts, Raju was rusticated from college and had remained an undergraduate, while she got married and had left for Oslo with her doctor husband. She had last seen Raju alive at the Railway Station, pulling his rickshaw along with other poor Faridabadis.

A month since the accident, Ravi Khanna—who had by now come to India and had been told the story about his wife's 'very good friend' from college—decided to adopt the poor seventeen-year-old boy. Ravi and Reema had everything in the world, except that they were childless. They mutually decided to adopt Rahul and give him a new lease of life. It was the best they could do to compensate for having taken his father's life.

Reema visited Rahul at his home where he had continued to live after his father's death, and when he saw her, he looked at her with despise. He would not talk to her, but when she told him about knowing his father very well and wanting to talk about the compensation, he let her in.

She told him the truth. She told him about her short-lived, close friendship with his father. She told him everything except the intimate moments that she had shared with Raju. She also told him that after the accident, she could not recognize Raju, who looked fragile and much older than his age. She told him that Ram Singh was a cover-up, that it was she who had been behind the wheel. She was the one who had killed his father, and that she was now desperate to do anything for him as repentance and as a mark of respect for the departed soul. She told him that if his father had not been imprisoned, she, in all probability, would have married Raju. Her words stunned Rahul. He sat there gaping at her, at a complete loss of words.

Reema was crying as she told him that God had definitely not been kind to Raju, but He had also kept her wanting all these years to have a child of her own. Without any hesitation, she told him that she somehow felt that Rahul was closest to being her child. She and her husband now wanted nothing more than to have him as their son and to take him along to Oslo, so they could give him the best of comforts and education.

Rahul thought for a while before speaking to her. He told her that his mother often rebuked his father about some college mate whom he kept referring to and was unable to forget. Rahul then took out an old wooden box from a trunk and opened it to show Reema the two-rupee notes that his father had neatly preserved as his most treasured possession. He told her that there were a lot of blanks he could not fill earlier but that now, after coming to know about his father's relationship with her, he was able to understand things clearly.

It took Reema numerous visits and a lot of convincing to have Rahul agree to go to Oslo with them. His anger slowly died out once he realized that the unfortunate incident was an accident, and he finally forgave Reema for what she had done unintentionally.

Dr Reema and Dr Ravi Khanna formally adopted Rahul and gave him their surname. They took him to Oslo where Rahul's life changed. He was provided with the best of luxuries and was made the heir apparent to their empire. In due course of time, the son of a rickshaw puller in Faridabad completed his medical degree from a college in Norway and went on to become a renowned cardiologist.

Reema began to spend a lot of time in Faridabad and became fully involved with the management of their hospitals. Dr Rahul Khanna decided to return to India and spend his life in Faridabad. He became the managing director of the Jeev-Daya Group of hospitals bought over by his parents and actively participated in running the chain in various tier-2 cities and converting them into modern state-of-the-art medical care centres. With the passage of time, these hospitals became some of the best in the country, providing the finest of medical services. The family ensured that no deaths took place for the need of proper medical facilities.

Reema and Rahul's relationship fell into a natural bond. The mother–son duo shared a special fondness for each other. However, the person to bring them together remained missing in their lives. Seeing him grow into a capable and confident person, Reema, to some extent, felt gratified that she had been in a position to help Raju's son. How could she ever forget the memorable moments of love and happiness she had shared with her closest friend? Rahul's progress pacified her and somewhat lessened the guilt in her heart.

Standing on her balcony in the Faridabad house, she smiled to herself, 'You will finally be with me through your son, O Rickshaw Faridabadi!'

A Ticklish Affair

After a major mishap on a cruiser, Krish goes down the memory lane to relive the years gone by and the extramarital affair that he had with Radhika. A chance meeting with her had a lasting effect on Krish, who had realized that it was neither a seven-year itch nor a passing attraction; it was something more than that. The attraction was somehow on both the sides, becoming an affaire de coeur.

Krish Seth stood on the top deck of the luxury liner, taking in deep breaths of the pure sea breeze. He was excited about the trip. He could feel the water breaking under him as the liner sailed forward, sending blue-white waves into the distance. The air was balmy. He closed his eyes. The swaying of the ship soothed him. He wished he could remain like this forever. Krish was glad that he had stuck to his decision of coming on this trip. His mind strayed to the last couple of months and he smiled to himself—though back then, informing his parents about his plans was an awkward situation. The senior Seths—Krish's parents—wanted to organize a lavish theme-party for their son and daughter-in-law on their twenty-fifth wedding anniversary. Krish and Sarika had been thrown off guard because they had been making their own plans. For years, they had been dreaming of going on a European Cruise on their silver wedding anniversary. It was with much trepidation that they had spoken to the parents of their plans, and luckily, for them, the parents had accepted wholeheartedly. However, many of their other relatives had not been so gracious.

Sarika now joined Krish on the deck and they laughed as they thought of the past weeks spent dodging family and friends who wanted to know how the couple was going to celebrate the occasion. There was disappointment all around when their near and dear ones were politely told that there was going to be no party. Krish and Sarika became busy with their research on selecting the right cruise. Of all the choices around the European region, they zeroed in on the Western Mediterranean Sea Cruises, because of the attractive sightseeing options, activities and facilities they offered.

After innumerable hours spent surfing the Internet and speaking to half a dozen travel agents, Sarika finally selected the Voyager—a cruise ship that was offering them a seven-day programme that began at Tunis, Tunisia, and ended at Barcelona, Spain, en route to the cities of Italy and France. Excited and impatient, the couple had been only too glad to embark upon their journey.

On 10 February 2015, once they had set foot on board the luxury liner, they could finally put all the preparations of the past few weeks behind. Now, it was only the two of them and their days ahead, and they wanted every bit to live their dream.

The first two days on the ship were spent exploring the plethora of facilities offered on board. They had a lovely cabin on the deck of the seventh-floor that had convenient access to the various activity and entertainment areas. Although small, it was comfortable and had a private balcony. The main dining hall was situated on the same floor and offered buffets for all meals. There were several restaurants on the ship catering to different cuisines, and at the entrance of these restaurants, a staff member was always present with a cleanser spray for cleaning the hands of the diners. From 5 p.m. to 6 p.m.—the 'Happy Hours'—food and drink concessions were offered to the passengers.

After dinner, there was music, dance and magic shows to entertain the passengers. The staff was courteous, caring and extremely attentive to all of the passengers' needs. Wonderful weather conditions prevailed, with clear skies and soft breeze, allowing the passengers a lot of time outdoors—lounging, swimming, playing sports or walking on the decks. Shore excursions were also very well-organized and well-guided. Krish and Sarika enjoyed the luxury that surrounded them, availing every experience possible. They even learned about the workings of the ship. And by the end of two days, they had become familiar with many of their co-passengers.

On the night of 12 February 2015—their anniversary—an open-air terrace, bedecked with fragrant flowers, under a star-studded sky, was selected as the party venue. A small group of specially invited guests graced the couple's special occasion, celebrated with a candlelight dinner. 'It was perfect,' thought Krish and Sarika, as they danced to a much-loved tune played by the live band. Sarika proposed that they come back for their fiftieth anniversary celebrations, and Krish sealed this agreement with a kiss. The group cheered on. It was the perfect night for their anniversary.

The Voyager sailed with 776 people on board, of which, 480 were passengers on their holidays, while 296 were crew and staff. The grand liner covered the cities of Rome and Florence, in Italy, and Marseilles, in Southern France.

A Ticklish Affair

It was the fifth day of their trip. The Voyager was between Spain's Majorca Islands and the Italian Island of Sardinia. As Krish and Sarika stood on the top deck watching the sea in the distance, the winds changed. The sky turned dark and a storm started to brew. The captain ran strict orders for all passengers to return to their cabins immediately and to remain indoors until further notice. He could portend, by the look of the sky, that the chance of a climate calamity was high. His hunch was right.

The storm hit within minutes. Giant waves, almost eighty feet high, lashed against the ship, smashing a bridge window and knocking the control systems out. Krish and Sarika had barely reached their deck when the ship lurched to one side. The air was filled with the sound of people screaming and objects falling. Fire extinguishers dislodged from their mounts and rolled across the floor. The staff were shouting instructions all around. Krish and Sarika saw men, women and children running towards the main dining hall. But the scene there was far from encouraging. Plates and glasses lay smashed on the floor. People slipped and slid, with water everywhere, as the ship swayed from side to side. The number of people in the dining hall increased. People were frightened out of their wits. Looking for some calm and comfort in the presence of their co-passengers, Krish and Sarika joined the others, too.

The ship jumped and pitched as the storm worsened. The captain's voice came over the public address system assuring the passengers that everything would be under control soon. But, even as he spoke, his voice was cut off due to power failure. The lights went out. People panicked. Someone shouted that they should get to the top deck, as the ship would surely sink. There was a stampede to exit the hall. Some were thrown against the fixed tables. There were cries of pain. Torches came on. The staff tried to calm everyone as they ran to help the women and children first. Amidst the confusion and chaos, members of families were separated. Krish tightly held on to Sarika's hand.

The ship's main machinery stopped, disabling its rudder. The captain and his crew could not control the ship anymore. They initiated transmission of distress signals out in the Mediterranean. A French cargo ship picked up the SOS calls first, followed by a British naval ship sailing close by, and these despatched rescue teams immediately. Trained naval officers in lifeboats began the evacuation of the passengers of the luxury liner.

It was only 4 p.m., but the sky was pitch dark as the thunderous storm continued to rage, with intermittent and fierce lightning. Krish and Sarika, covered with cuts and bruises, were given life jackets and bundled into a lifeboat. The sea was rough and the waves high. The conditions were exceedingly difficult even for the experienced seamen conducting the rescue operation. The rescue boats were steered towards Sardinia, the nearest port. Two tugs were also despatched to haul the luxury liner out of the sea.

Krish, suddenly remembering something, instinctively checked his pockets. Was he carrying his wallet or had he left it in his cabin? After an anxious search, he managed to extricate the article from under his life jacket and fall back in his seat, relieved. He took out a piece of paper from the inner flap of the wallet, and holding it close to his heart, he began to pray. The paper boat in his hand had always given him luck and a feeling of safety. Someone important had given it to him, her last words being, 'Keep this with you. It will take you out of troubled waters in my absence.' He was also amazed that even under these circumstances, his memory of her had come back to him so clearly.

Immediately, the storm began to subside as if by a miracle. To everyone's surprise, the skies cleared and the waters calmed down. It became easier for the lifeboats to steer the passengers to safety where ambulances and nursing staff awaited them. The passengers were given first aid, a hot meal and a place to rest.

After more than ten hours of sleep, Krish woke up to find himself on a comfortable bed in a hotel room. Turning, he found his wife fast asleep. Their luggage had been delivered to their room. A note informed him that the French-led rescue operation had been a timely one and that the liner had been hauled to safety. No lives were lost. Relieved, he got out of bed and made coffee for himself. He went out to the balcony of the room and found a deck-recliner. It looked heavenly. He sat, half-reclining, facing the expanse of the blue sea. Sipping his drink, he took out his wallet again. His fingers felt the frayed paper of the boat and his heart thanked the person who had given it to him. It had saved his life—literally taking him out of troubled waters.

Sitting on the recliner, now completely relaxed and at peace with himself, her memory came back to Krish. It was the winter of 1992 in Delhi when he had first seen her...

She was walking down the stairs of a commercial complex, and as her feet skipped on each step, her flowing hair bounced about her shoulders, matching her gait. Strikingly good-looking, she surpassed all the conventional parameters of beauty. She was fair, had high cheekbones, sharp features—a face that commanded second glances. Her doe-shaped eyes shone brightly with joy. She was the most beautiful girl Krish had ever seen. She looked around for something, and then he saw her walking into a shop to use the telephone.

Krish stood mesmerized. Something about her had struck a

chord in him. He suddenly realized that he was standing in the middle of the complex staring at her. She finished her phone call and walked past him, oblivious to the admiring gazes all around. She was engrossed in her own thoughts. 'With looks like that, she would be accustomed to such glances,' he thought. He continued to stare at her when he felt a tap on his shoulder. It was his wife Sarika.

It took him several moments to realize where he was. He was there to pick his wife up from her office. Sarika noticed the embarrassed look on her husband's face as he tried to recover from being caught red-handed. She laughed mischievously and said, 'My dear husband, that attractive girl you were ogling at happens to be my replacement during my six-month maternity leave. My company's director has just appointed her.'

'Six months?' Krish almost yelled, astonished. 'That long?! I can't take even a day off from my own advertising agency if I want to keep it open.' Getting into the car, she smiled, 'Darling, that's what you think. It's all in your mind. Learn to run your company without being there all the time micro managing your employees. Learn to delegate.'

Krish might have argued, but his mind was filled with that amazing girl who had, only a few minutes ago, passed by him like a breath of fresh air. As casually as he could, he asked Sarika the name of the girl.

'Radhika!' She replied. Krish drove on, the name playing on his mind. 'Radhika… What a lovely name! It suits her.' Sarika did not read much into her husband's reaction or behaviour. Looks like those of Radhika's naturally drew such attention.

Sarika was also an attractive girl—confident, carefree, a pleasing personality and very pretty. She was as happy in her home and family life as she was with her job as an HR in a multinational company. She made a loving wife and Krish doted on her.

For many days thereafter, Krish's mind kept wandering back to Radhika. 'What a beautiful girl', he would think, and then drag himself back to his work. 'Would he ever see her again?' he wondered. It was sooner than he could have imagined. He had promised to take his school friends to dinner at Parikrama—The Revolving Restaurant that had newly opened on the twenty-fifth floor of Antriksh Bhawan in Connaught Place. Krish and Sarika, along with their guests, were at the end of their meal when he saw her walking in. She was accompanied by her husband and an older couple. Krish froze. She looked even prettier than before, and just like the previous time, he seemed to lose his bearings. With difficulty, he kept his attention on his guests, although he kept glancing furtively in her direction every now and again. He lost sight of her behind a pillar as the restaurant revolved and when she came into view again, he was shocked to see her walking up to their table, a smile on her face. Of course, she was coming to meet his wife! Sarika introduced Radhika to the others at the table. Krish stammered something incoherent. After a short exchange of pleasantries, she returned to her table, and to everyone's surprise, Krish ordered another round of dessert.

The chance meeting had a lasting effect on Krish. He kept hoping for more encounters, and they did occur. A few weeks later, Krish and Sarika were at a theatre in Mandi House when they ran into Radhika and her husband, Naveen. They exchanged greetings and took their seats. Krish found himself unable to concentrate on the play they had come to watch. He kept glancing sideways in Radhika's direction. He gulped, 'Was she too looking at them? Had she noticed him eyeing her? Maybe she was beginning to get amused at his silly reactions every time they met?' He could not stop himself from thinking about her.

After the meeting at the theatre, Krish began to pick up his wife from her office much more frequently, just so he could get a glimpse of Radhika. Sarika still had a few days of office and Krish took full advantage of the situation. 'It was just a fancy I would soon get over,' Krish told himself. 'It was just a passing attraction!' But his heart felt something beyond his own understanding.

A few weeks later, Sarika gave birth to a beautiful baby girl and the Seth family was thrilled. Sarika was now on maternity leave to nurse her little baby. They named her Kritika. Krish would have loved to name the little one Radhika, but that would have been going too far. He did not even have the courage to suggest it. One evening, on his return home, he was pleasantly surprised by the presence of colleagues from Sarika's office; they were visiting to wish the new mother. Radhika was one of them. She played with his Kritika, who was now two months old. She had brought some baby dresses. Krish noticed that Sarika had grown quite fond of Radhika and that the two had become good friends.

He had to admit to himself that he could not get her out of his mind. This was no passing attraction. Not anymore. It had to be something deeper, because he had never felt this way about anyone before. He was not sure how he was going to deal with his feelings. He tried to reason with himself, 'How could he even think of her as anything more than his wife's colleague? And why would she be noticing him when she had a handsome husband who worked in the merchant navy? They made a great couple and Radhika looked content in every way.' Krish checked himself. Why was he even thinking this way? He promised himself not to give in to his emotions and to prevent his feelings from getting the better of him. So, Krish busied himself with his work and his little daughter, and was his usual self again. This was until the time one of Sarika's colleagues invited them to his wedding.

Not very comfortable with driving back alone late at night from a Gurugram hotel, Radhika arranged with Sarika to accompany them to the wedding venue. Later, they could drop her off to her residence, which was incidentally very close to the Seth's in Delhi. Krish found himself selecting his most expensive suit for the occasion. He wished to look his best and he was glad he did, because when Radhika walked in, he could only gape. Dressed in an embroidered traditional saree, with jewellery to match, she looked gorgeous. His heart raced as he drove to the venue, blood gushing in his veins. On the one hand, he felt ecstatic to have her with them; on the other hand, he became disheartened and quiet. Sarika and Radhika even commented on his lack of interest in their conversation, but Krish could not help it. He was just not himself.

The evening was not an easy one. His spirits further dampened when some male colleagues began talking about Radhika, and how they had nicknamed her the 'Beauty Queen' of the company. It hurt him to hear them talk this way, and he refused to be served any liquor for fear that he might lose his control and react. He also had the responsibility of driving his two women back. Later in the evening, somehow, he compelled himself to enjoy the occasion, and on the drive back, he was in a lighter frame of mind and freely engaged in conversation with Radhika, who seemed to enjoy talking, too. There were continuous discussions between them, while Sarika sat back and relaxed after her quota of vodka. Her mind was on Kritika, as this was the first time she had left her daughter back home with Krish's parents. Suddenly, she requested that she be dropped home first, and then Krish could drop Radhika at her residence.

When Sarika got off, Radhika took the front seat. Krish's mind began racing again. This was his chance to get to know her better, to know what she thought of him. 'Your house is very far Radhika, I know a shortcut via India Gate that will get us there faster,' he blurted. Radhika turned around to look at him, wondering how India Gate figured in their route. 'What?' She asked, and burst out laughing. She looked at the time on the dashboard. 'Well, why not?' She agreed. 'I'd love a drive at this hour with no traffic.' He was pleasantly surprised.

They chatted non-stop, finding a lot of things in common between them. Krish drove to India Gate through the wide and landscaped roads of Chanakyapuri. He found a lone ice cream vendor, bought two favourites, and left a heavy tip for the shocked man. Clearly, Krish's spirits were soaring high. The two sat in the parked car, enjoying their ice cream, continuing to share their stories. He talked of his beautiful memories of his school and college days in Delhi. She, being new to the city—having lived there only until she was four—enjoyed his reminiscing. She was from Pune and had completed her studies from there. As he dropped her off at her gate, she thanked him and offered her hand. He held it a shade longer than necessary. She smiled—a smile he knew he would never forget. Nor would he forget that night. It was the most romantic night of his life. It was 4 a.m. when he tiptoed into his bedroom. He could not sleep. All that had transpired that night, kept playing in his mind in a loop.

The next day—Monday—Krish was very distracted in office. He refused to meet any clients. At lunchtime, he made a decision and called up Sarika's office. Only this time, he asked for Radhika. They talked for a long time, thanking each other for the previous night.

Krish had been busy with his work in his advertising office, but he could not stop his mind from wandering. Three days later, a courier service delivered a packet for him—a neatly wrapped Sheaffer pen with a note that read, 'Thank you for the drive'. Krish held the pen as though it were the most precious thing in the world. He tried it, jotting down a few lines and realized his writing matched hers on the note.

That evening, long after his staff had left for the day, he sat by his office window thinking. Krish had always believed that he was more than content with his life. He had everything he could ask for. So what was this new sense of joy that now filled his heart?

That week, Radhika had some official work that took her past Krish's office. He invited her for a cup of tea on her return. She liked the decor of his office, the hustle-bustle and the music that played in the background. When he closed his office, Krish offered to drop her home. They talked at length as he drove around in circles. He went via the Ridge Road and called it a 'long-cut'. That had her laughing. Radhika was very happy and her usual chirpy self and Krish wondered how he too felt so light in her company. She began teasing him. Pointing to pink and magenta bougainvillea along the way, she challenged him to spell the name of the flower. But Krish kept missing out one letter or another. 'If you spell "bougainvillea", you can have me right here,' Radhika laughed. Krish now tried even harder, but was unsuccessful. Completely engrossed in the conversation, Krish did not notice a truck approaching from a blind turn. He swerved just in time, but the close save had Radhika screaming and she reached out for him. Badly shaken, she held on to him tightly. Krish stopped the car on the lonely road to calm her down. He was shaking, too. They held each other as Krish held her head against his shoulder. Suddenly, he bent down and kissed her. Moments later, Radhika pushed him away, and they drove to her house in an awkward silence. They parted without speaking, neither knowing what to say.

Days after this incident, in the midst of Delhi monsoon, Radhika was caught in a commercial hub and could not reach her car parked some distance away. She ran for shade, but got completely drenched in the process. As luck would have it, Krish had also taken the same shelter. Both exchanged glances and stood, waiting. Krish glanced at her, but Radhika kept her eyes away, not meeting his. After that kiss, he longed to talk to her, to take her in his arms and tell her everything would be fine. Finally, he decided to walk up to her. He suggested that they go to his office nearby, dry themselves there and have a cup of tea. They needed to talk, he said, and the rain would subside by then. She accepted, and together they walked to his office. There was no one in the office, the staff having left for the day. He handed her a towel, and they wiped themselves as best they could. One thing led to another and they found themselves in each other's arms without realizing what was happening.

The physical intimacy changed everything. Guilt flooded them. Radhika had tears in her eyes. 'What is going on Krish? Is this right?' she asked.

'I am very attracted to you, Radhika, and I can't seem to help it. I have tried, but I can't stay away.' Krish felt relieved pouring his heart out. For a moment, she was quiet. He held his breath till she said, 'I can understand. I feel the same.' But Krish knew it was not right. How could he tell her it was!

And without a thought, he said, 'How can I hurt my family? They come first.'

She retorted, 'My family comes first, too.'

The conversation ended abruptly. Krish chided himself for bringing his family in. They could have settled the matter in some other way but it was too late now. Just then, there was a call from Sarika asking why he was still in office.

'In a meeting,' said Krish, feeling miserable for lying.

Radhika was still sobbing when he walked her to her car. Krish was at a loss.

He had gotten himself into a ticklish situation.

For a few days they did not speak. Finally, Krish gave her a call, but she would not speak to him. He sent her a bottle of perfume with a note that read, 'Falling in love with you was the second best thing in the world for me; finding you was the first.' She did not respond right away, but after a few days, called him asking to meet.

They decided to handle the situation in a mature way. There was absolutely no reason to disturb their families. She extracted a promise from him that they would not let any physical intimacy occur between them ever again. They were happily married, disliked the word 'affair' and only circumstances had led to what had happened on Ridge Road. Almost being in a gruesome accident had unnerved them, leading to the closeness, they reasoned.

From that day, their friendship took a backseat.

For many months, Radhika and Krish did not speak to each other. One day, Sarika invited Radhika over for lunch. Krish's parents also joined the women at the dining table. A normal conversation followed and Krish's mother, Mrs Seth, asked Radhika about her childhood in Delhi. Radhika told her that her family had stayed at Babar Road in Bengali Market. This took Mrs Seth by surprise because in the 1970s her family too had stayed in the same location. She asked Radhika what her maiden name was. When Radhika said 'Mehra', the senior Seths exclaimed. Tears welled up Mrs Seth's eyes and Mr Seth stopped eating. Sarika and Radhika were astonished at such a reaction. Mrs Seth had a lump in her throat. Wiping her eyes, she asked Radhika, 'Are you my little doll? Is your nickname Dolly?'

Radhika was stunned. Mrs Seth, half laughing, half crying, told Radhika that the Mehra's had been their neighbours and that the two families were very close to each other. 'We were the best of friends with your parents during the seven years of their stay at Babar Road. I was present when you were born in Dr Sen's Nursing Home. You looked like a doll so I started calling you "Dolly" from the very first day. The name stuck and everyone called you by that name until you went to school. Your father worked for Chartered Bank at that time and he was transferred to London. You were only six then. The distance separated us and we lost contact.' Mrs Seth finished tearfully, as she came around the table and hugged Radhika as if she had found a long-lost daughter.

Tears filled Radhika's eyes, too. An age-old relationship had existed between the families. Krish's parents talked about the good old times and Radhika added to their stories based on what she had heard from her parents. It was a wonderful reunion after two decades.

After having some tea, Radhika left their home. She drove slowly, her mind racing through everything she had just learned. She vividly remembered her mother telling her that, when she was six years old, her parents had mutually decided with Krish's parents that they would get them both married when they grew up. Both the families had come very close and wanted to convert their friendship into a relationship. It suddenly dawned on Radhika that her name had been derived from 'Radha'; because of Krishan, Krish's full name.

It all seemed like divine intervention. 'Was this why I was so drawn towards him?' Radhika wondered, smiling to herself. She wanted to reach home and call up her parents to give them the astonishing news. Her mind went to Krish: 'Oh, how I'd love to see his reaction when he hears of this!'

Krish was in a state of complete disbelief. Could it be true that she was his long-lost childhood friend? He wanted to process all that he had heard, but his mind was clouded by memories of the past. He told his secretary to cancel all his official appointments. He was not to be disturbed, not even telephone calls. He locked himself in his cabin, needing time to comprehend the meaning of this new development. The axis of his little world had suddenly shifted.

He sat on his sofa with his head in his palms, slowly remembering his childhood days at Babar Road, with Dolly, his first love. Gradually, the hazy memories of the days gone by became clearer. He remembered the little six-year-old girl with whom he used to play. It was no wonder that he had felt a bond every time he saw her. 'Unbelievable!' was all he could think. He felt an urgent need to talk to her. His hands were trembling as he picked up the telephone. All he managed to ask her was, 'What have you to say about this twist in our story?'

She replied, 'I didn't want to talk over the phone. I wanted to see your reaction in person.'

But he continued, 'Do you realize that had your family not shifted to the UK, we would have grown up together and even gotten married?'

'Yes, that would have solved our problem. And what do you have to say to this?'

'I think God wants us to meet,' was his reply.

'So let's meet, then,' said Radhika.

She reached his office. He was waiting outside, impatient and extremely excited. Her eyes were sparkling and unmindful of the people around, Radhika hugged him. Krish drove them to a hotel where he had reserved a room. He led her to the thirteenth floor and she followed without questioning him. Once they were within the comfort of the closed doors, they held each other instinctively. They had so much to say, yet, they could not exchange a single word. They kissed wildly, both wanting to get closer than was humanly possible. They were lost in the sea of their emotions with no inhibitions holding them back. After what seemed like an hour, Krish and Radhika came back to their senses. She got out of bed and made them tea. He spoke for the first time, 'Hello Dolly!' She came and sat beside him, and looking into his eyes, said, 'I couldn't wait to tell you. Just this morning, when I was looking at myself in the mirror, what I saw was your face, Krish.' He looked at her and then pulled her back into his arms.

They talked, reminiscing twenty years back to 1972. Some memories were crystal clear, others they had to strain their minds to remember. Krish, being older, had more to share. He remembered the time when he was almost nine-years-old and had learnt to ride a bicycle. It had impressed the six-year-old Dolly. Time stood still as they conversed.

From this point on, they stopped questioning the relationship, believing that all was destined. Radhika now visited Krish's house frequently, often staying back for a meal with his parents. They treated her as their own daughter, one whom they were most delighted to have back in their lives. Krish, Sarika and Radhika became regular companions. They sought each other out for their various outings. Whether it was for a meal at a restaurant, a movie, or a play they wanted to watch, they were always together. In fact, not only Radhika, but her husband Naveen also became an inseparable part of the Seth family. And Krish and Radhika only grew closer. They shared emotional as well as physical intimacy that they assumed was only a natural follow-through to the deep connection they had earlier felt for each other. As long as they prioritized their families above all else, they believed their relationship was justified. It was always meant to be, and they were doing no one any harm.

Once Sarika joked, 'Isn't it strange? In today's modern times, Radha and Krishan have become sister and brother to each other!' Krish and Radhika exchanged a quick glance, trying to put up a brave smile. But that comment churned something deep within them. It further established the intense bond they felt for each other.

But life was not going to allow the two to continue this way. One day, they had to face the consequences of their actions. At a party that Sarika had thrown for her colleagues, Krish got drunk and dragged Radhika to the dance floor. He could not keep his hands off her, and what surprised everyone was that Radhika also did not object. Embarrassed and shocked, Sarika and Naveen turned away in silence. But later, once they were back home, the two demanded an explanation. Sarika was furious. How could her husband behave that way, that too in front of her colleagues? And with Radhika? 'What is the meaning of this?' But not much could be resolved with a drunk Krish and a crying Radhika.

The two couples met the next morning. A sober Krish

apologized as best as he could. He swore never to consume liquor again. Radhika tried to convince Sarika that whatever had happened the night before was entirely meaningless. They were in a lively mood and were just having fun. She had already tried explaining her behaviour to her husband. But to no avail. The damage had been done. The relationship between the two couples turned sour and they parted ways. Of the four, Naveen had the least to say. He blamed himself for having joked with his wife about having a girlfriend at every port. He held himself responsible for being away for long stretches of time.

Four months passed without any contact between the families. Then one morning, Krish received a call from Radhika. She wanted to talk. She asked him to meet her for lunch at Parikrama.

She was subdued, nervous and not her cheerful self. Krish could see that she was having trouble saying what she had come to tell him. She remained silent for a while, fidgeting. After a while, she informed him that her husband had resigned from his merchant navy assignment. He had taken a new job with Star Cruise in Singapore and they were going to relocate to their new country of residence very soon. Radhika said, 'I can't see our relationship going any further.' And she thanked him for being a part of her life.

Krish felt like a ton of bricks had fallen on his head. He sat there staring at her, completely lost for words. Heaviness filled his heart. He had kept the hope alive that someday, things would be well between them and he would have his Radha back. But it seemed it was not to be. They ordered a light lunch and nibbled through it, neither noticing what they were eating. They were just prolonging what they knew was going to be their final moments together. He noticed how beautiful she was, just like the first time he had seen her. What a coincidence that she was introduced to him in this very restaurant. Was it a coincidence or did she want it that way, he wondered.

Radhika picked up a flyer lying on the table and absentmindedly started playing with it. Before she knew it, she had made a boat with it. She looked at it thoughtfully, and then she reached for his hand and opening his palm, placing the little object there. She closed his hand, but left her hand on his.

'Keep this with you,' she said softly. 'This boat will take you out of troubled waters in my absence.' Tears filled her eyes. Krish let her hand be for a while and then taking the precious boat, he kept it carefully in his wallet, never to lose it.

It was time to go different ways. In parting, Krish's voice choked as he said, 'Walking alone was not difficult. But when we have walked miles together, being back alone is going to be very difficult.' He wished her well in her life. And then, they said their final farewell. The beginning and ending at the revolving restaurant seemed to imply that their lives with each other had taken a full circle.

The sound of the hooter from the French ship anchored in the sea shook him out of his reverie. He looked at the worn out boat in his hand once more and then placed it back in his wallet. It would remain his anchor for as long as possible, giving him the strength he needed. So what if it were only made of paper, it had weathered many of life's storms and steered him to safety as it carried the strength of someone's profound wishes.

Their relationship would always remain precious. After all, it was an affaire de coeur (a true matter of the heart).

The Kikar Tree

A real-life incident, which occurred in the Seekar area of Rajasthan, when a poor farmer, attacked by a predator, somehow escaped from the jaws of death by climbing the lone Kikar tree. The incident was later misused by an absconder-turned-spiritual guru to fill the coffers.

It is indeed a revelation for those who blindly believe the so-called, self-styled gurus and their false propaganda. The magical tricks played by them to lure innocent people, with a religious bent of mind, are highlighted in this story.

This story has been taken by the trustees of Immaculate Ideal Human Foundation to be made into a film and would be released shortly. The film would be made by the producer of the famous film Grihalakshmi: The Awakening.

Ramhet Meena was a poor farmer who lived with his family in Kutalpura Maliyan—a village situated a short distance from the tenth-century Ranthambore Fort that lay within the Ranthambore National Park in Sawai Madhopur District, Rajasthan. The villagers in the area depended upon the tourists who visited the fort ruins as well as the National Park that was famous for its tiger sightings, for their livelihood.

One day, on his way back home in a bus, Ramhet was in

a cheerful mood, humming a folk song to himself. He had just sold a truckload of guava, cultivated by him, for a whopping sum of thirty-seven thousand rupees at the Sawai Madhopur Mandi. It was the highest bidding price he had ever got in the main market. He kept touching the bag in which he carried the money, but then, realizing that this would attract the attention of his co-passengers, he stopped himself from doing so.

The Rajasthan Roadways bus was still ten kilometres from the village when its axle suddenly gave way. It was not the road that was to blame, but the pitiable condition of the bus itself. Most buses being plied on these routes went for decades without proper maintenance by the state-run department. The vehicle came to a sudden halt. The driver cursed loudly and threw his hands in the air in sheer exasperation. The poor passengers realized that the bus had finally met its end on that road.

While the other commuters chose to wait for the next bus that was expected to arrive in an hour, from the nearby town of Sawai Madhopur, Ramhet Meena decided to walk through the vast, semi-barren fields towards his small village. Though he was aware that it was risky to walk alone at that time of the evening when the sun was about to set, no untoward incident had occurred in the recent past, and that made him confident. He knew the area well and thought that if his steps were quick enough, he would reach his village before it got dark. The sun was slowly setting behind the hill of the royal ruins of the fort, which was one of the highest forts in the entire Rajasthan belt of the Aravalli Hills.

Ramhet took off across the fields. He strode as fast as he could, even breaking into a jog from time to time. He had walked this route earlier as well, but had always been accompanied by four or five other villagers. Being in a group kept predators at bay. In half an hour, he had covered half the distance. He spotted the foothill of the fort at a distance, with its dense forest, and quickened his pace. His bag not only contained the sale proceeds, but also the dress materials and bangles that he had bought for his wife and three daughters. He was eager to hand over the gifts to them. They wanted to wear new clothes for the 'ghoomar' dance festival at the holy Ganesh Temple on Ganesh Chaturthi. The birth of Lord Ganesh was to be celebrated within the temple compound next week.

A tiger had been wandering on the edge of the forest that surrounded the fort. It stood behind the thick foliage, not yet stepping forward onto the plain field. Ramhet, unaware of the danger that lurked amidst the trees, continued to walk as fast as he could even as the tiger readied itself for the kill, its hungry eyes staring at its prey. Suddenly, a troop of langurs, jumping from tree to tree, began to grunt, terrified by the presence of the tiger. Ramhet, familiar with the warning signals of the animals, immediately stopped where he was. He could not see the predator yet, but he stood holding his breath. A movement in the distance caught his attention, and he sighted the black and yellow stripes. Without wasting any time, he began to run. From the corner of his eye, he saw the tiger come out from behind the tree and charge in his direction.

The fields were mostly barren land, with patches of bushes and a lone kikar tree. In this landscape, Ramhet realized that he was no match for the giant tiger. The uneven ground was of no help either, so he dropped the heavy bag and kept running for his life. Soon, his muscles began to ache, and he became breathless, but he did not stop. The tiger was gaining ground, and Ramhet only had a few seconds to save himself. He was close to the kikar tree now. He thought of his wife and daughters, and that somehow gave him the extra power to try harder to save himself.

The hungry beast was gaining quickly now. Ramhet used all his strength to reach the tree. He had barely managed to climb a bit when the animal lunged forward, paws outstretched, missing Ramhet's feet by a whisker. He climbed higher and held on to a sturdy branch, continuing to look down as he did.

The tiger, all 12-feet of him, made another attempt to reach for its prey, shaking the tree as it fell against the trunk. Luckily, for Ramhet, he was safely out of reach.

Ramhet realized he had hurt himself. In his scramble up the thorny tree, he had suffered deep gashes over his knee, cuts over his arms and acute pain in one ankle, which was probably sprained. But he was relieved and thanked God for keeping him safe, at least for the moment. He looked around, wondering if he could call for help, but in that wilderness, there was nobody in sight. A tree in the midst of that desolate field was a miracle in itself.

The tiger walked around the tree, frustrated at having missed what was a sure meal. After some time, it sat down against the trunk and growled, sending shivers up Ramhet's spine.

Ramhet began shouting for help at the top of his voice. He was aware that it was of no use. No one was going to hear him out there at this time of the evening, and yet, he screamed again and again. He cursed his decision to walk alone when he knew that there were wild beasts in the National Park. By now, it was getting dark. Tears rolled down Ramhet's eyes. Except for the half-moon in the sky, there was nothing else in sight. The tiger stayed where it was, glancing up now and again towards the helpless man on the tree.

By midnight, Ramhet was exhausted. Looking down, he

could see the tiger lying across, its head resting on its front paws. He kept praying that it would give up and leave, but there was no movement from the animal. There was nothing to do but wait for daylight. Ramhet settled himself on the upper branches. He took off his kurta and turban and tied his legs and waist to the branches to secure himself. He could barely close his eyes for even a second, but he did not want to take any chances with falling off. In any case, thorns pricked him all over his body, preventing him from getting any rest. He could feel blood oozing from deep cuts in his arms. He used the leaves, whose medicinal properties he was well aware of, to clean his wounds. He thought of his family and how worried they would be by now.

As the sky started to lighten, he was extremely thirsty as well as exhausted. The tiger was still there sound asleep. The branches and leaves were not enough to provide shade to the tiger. It began to stir uncomfortably because of the direct sunlight. Suddenly, it noticed the movement of a pack of deer at the outskirts of the forest. Hungry as it was, the tiger gave a last look towards the treetop and left for the forest, disappearing behind the trees. Ramhet heard the grunting of the langurs once again and heaved a sigh of relief. He, however, waited for a little longer before getting down from the tree. His bruises hurt and he could not put his full weight on his twisted ankle, but he slowly walked towards where he had thrown his bag, looking over his shoulder now and again. He managed to retrieve his treasure and then he made his way home.

The local doctor immediately attended to Ramhet after which his family members and some of the villagers gathered around him. He narrated the entire incident to them much to the shock of his parents, wife and children. His wife Padmavati wept as she listened to her husband's ordeal and cursed the tiger. 'God be praised for the kikar tree,' she said at the end of the tale, 'If it were not for the tree, he would not have escaped the claws of the wild tiger.'

After a couple of weeks when Ramhet had recovered from the trauma, an auspicious day was chosen, and the entire Meena clan went to the site of the incident. They offered their prayers to the kikar tree. They carried various articles on a large tray such as holy water, fruits, vermillion, sacred thread and scented candles for their ritual. Padmavati led the prayers, overwhelmed as she was by the presence of the tree that had saved her from becoming a widow.

While the group offered their prayers, villagers walking towards Sawai Madhopur saw the small contingent of Ramhet Meena from afar. They assumed that this was a sacred tree, and soon news of it spread quickly in the entire district. People started going to the kikar tree to offer their obeisance and tie the sacred thread, wondering how they had not been aware of it until then. The word spread that if one prayed to the Tree God, one's wishes would come true. Coincidentally, some people did receive what they had prayed for, and stories of this wish-granting tree spread far and wide. Devotees began to throng the site of the once-ignored tree in the middle of that vast semi-barren land.

A sect run by Guru Dev Singh Solanki also heard the news of the kikar tree. The guru was wise, cunning and shrewd. He understood that the tree had become famous due to some obscure reason. He assembled his disciples, and the troop left for the site to offer their prayers before the sacred tree.

The guru had no formal education but knew of the weaknesses of the poor, uneducated and superstitious inhabitants of the small villages in and around Sawai Madhopur. He recognized the opportunity to extract money from them. He would give hope to the poor and make them poorer. He initiated the construction of a small temple, dedicated to Lord Shiva at the site and spread the rumour that the tree was thousands of years old and that Lord Shiva had himself spent a night under it. He also announced that anyone who worshipped the sacred tree would get what they wished for.

The guru decided to perform a havan (prayer ceremony) and asked his disciples to spread the word around. During the ceremony that took place in front of hundreds of villagers, he broke a coconut. Milk and prasad (a devotional offering made to god) came out of it, and later, it caught fire. He then mysteriously took out another coconut from inside his robe and placed it on the floor. It began to move by itself. The villagers stood in awe and complete admiration. They believed that the guru had divine powers and could achieve any act if he willed it. They listened as he proclaimed that miracles happened around the kikar tree at night, and that Lord Shiva had spoken to him in a vision regarding the sanctity of the spot. He concluded the ritual by asking all those present to make their offerings. The more they offered, in money or in kind, the more the blessings they would get.

In the following months, the guru sent his emissaries to purchase land around the kikar tree and proceeded to build an ashram around the Lord Shiva temple. He and his disciples now lived and conducted their activities from there.

As time passed, the number of his followers increased manifold and people visited the district, especially to meet the guru who was now known as 'Kikar Guru'. Ramhet witnessed the phenomenal rise of the godman, and it did not take him long to understand why the kikar tree had begun to have a religious significance. He himself was the reason for it, and so was his wife, who had given so much importance to the tree and idolized it. He decided that he had to do something about it. He went to Mohan Singh Jalawar, police inspector of Sawai Madhopur District, and told him the whole story of what had actually happened and how the Guru was now taking undue advantage of the beliefs of the poor people.

Inspector Jalawar recognized this godman immediately. The self-proclaimed saint was, in reality, undergoing trial in Uttar Pradesh (UP) for the rape and murder of one of his foreign disciples. The inspector heard Ramhet out keenly, taking detailed notes, starting from the incident with the tiger, to the developments that followed, leading up to the havan performed recently by the guru. Ramhet also told the police officer about a discourse by the guru that he had recently attended. Hundreds of followers had gathered, and the guru had talked to his audience of the meaning of the word 'saint'. He had said: 'He/she is a person who is an ascetic, close to God, and one who does pious and righteous deeds in his or her life. Saints have special powers and live life in accordance with the theories propounded by Gautam Buddha, the Bhagavad Gita and other religions. They lend a healing touch to others' miseries and are bereft of any greed or wealth. They embrace all religions.'

The guru then told the audience that saints such as Gautam Buddha and Guru Nanak Dev belonged to a foregone era. In the current times, but for a few godmen, most were not capable of even preaching religious sermons. He asked his audience to be very careful in whom they laid their trust and added that they consider him their true guru.

Ramhet told the inspector how he had been spellbound

by the oratory skills of the guru, but the inspector was not impressed. He informed Ramhet that in his previous stint in UP, he had encountered a few such godmen who had a following of thousands of disciples, but who, from close quarters, were nothing more than average street magicians. They used their skills to fool innocent and superstitious people in the name of God.

The Guru that Ramhet spoke about was, in fact, a vagabond and a proclaimed offender. The UP police were after him. It was because of the high religious fervour prevalent in the state, that one could not apprehend him without substantial evidence of fraud. But there had been a build-up of cases, and so, the guru had moved lock, stock and barrel to Rajasthan.

Inspector Mohan had once visited the godman's ashram in UP in disguise. There, an elderly woman had casually started a conversation with him. Being well conversant with the tricks of the trade, the inspector had given the woman some wrong information about himself. He had told her that he was a transporter. He was unhappy because he had no children. When he met the so-called saint, the latter tried to impress him with his powers, saying that he knew that the visitor was connected to the transport business and was childless.

Mohan denied all of this categorically and rebutted the Guru's claim, who then pretended to have it all mixed up because he was getting old. A disciple suddenly intervened and reminded the Guru about his vow to begin his maunvrat (keeping silent). Taking the hint, the saint abruptly asked Mohan to leave. The inspector had recently been transferred from UP to Rajasthan and wanted to expose the fraud godman. In fact, he had been planning a detailed investigation on the guru when Ramhet had approached him with his revelations.

The inspector proposed that Ramhet be part of the team

assigned to investigate the activities of the ashram. He suggested that they join the ashram, pretending to be disciples of the guru. Ramhet Meena readily agreed. Two weeks later, the two of them, along with a media person, joined the society of Shiv Bhakts, and began to live in the ashram.

They followed a strict routine along with two hundred other ashramites (people staying at the ashram). Their day started at 3 a.m. to attend the morning prayers lead by the guru. Yoga followed, from 5 a.m. to 7 a.m., and after their breakfast, they went back to sleep. They were woken up by a gong at noon for a havan that the guru performed in a part of the ashram made especially for the purpose. After the ritual, the guru gave a discourse.

Either a topic was raised by one of his disciples selected on the spot or from an anonymous letter, from someone seeking guidance, was read out before him. At 1 p.m., the gong indicated lunchtime. Between 2.30 p.m. and 4.30 p.m., the ashramites met and interacted with each other. Then they gathered in the assembly hall to listen to the various problems raised by the local villagers. The guru gave quick solutions in the form of vibhuti (a holy powder). At 7 p.m., the disciples went to their respective chambers to sleep so they could wake up again at 3 a.m.

The inspector, Ramhet and the media person, under pseudonyms, began to closely observe the routines of the ashram. What they discovered right away was an interesting daily practice where a group of select ashram disciples were asked to disguise themselves as villagers and mingle with the ordinary people who came from various parts of the country.

When these people reached the ashram to have a darshan (visit) of the saint, they were ushered into a waiting hall where the chosen disciples gained their confidence by sharing their own fake problems with the visitors over a seemingly casual conversation. The unsuspecting victims would, in turn, share their purpose for visiting—their desires or problems in life. The information obtained was passed on to the Kikar Guru in the innermost chamber, which was well decorated and heavily guarded. The disciples also pressed upon the visitors the virtues and powers of the holy saint and their personal supernatural experiences with him.

The table was set, and the victims would be sent to the Guru. They would be amazed when he spoke of their problems without their uttering even a single word. The charismatic and shrewd godman would assess their state of mind and predict a date and time by when their miseries would end. They would leave, convinced of the superhuman powers that the Kikar Guru possessed.

The investigating team also figured out that the discourses that the Guru gave on selected topics were never extempore. He chose the topics himself and prepared the matter thoroughly beforehand. The innocent public would marvel at how learned he was and how he could speak on any topic—religious or otherwise.

There was an arrangement made by the inspector, wherein, an officer from the department, in the guise of a commoner, would periodically visit the trio in the ashram. At the end of the first week, he passed on samples of the vibhuti that the Guru gave out. This was to be tested to determine its composition. He also handed over the coconut, for a thorough examination. The vibhuti and coconut kernels were kept in an inner chamber in the ashram where certain activities were carried out by a close group of disciples that the rest of them were not privy to. In the days to come, the trio managed to unearth several fraudulent activities that went on in the ashram.

The guru had become famous for his ability to sing religious sermons. He was also known to make ducks dance. The actual truth was that he would tie the ducks on a tin plate covered with a dark cloth. He kept heaters under the plate. By the time the chanting of bhajans (devotional songs) reached its peak, the plates would be very hot, and the ducks would not be able to stand. The birds would continuously move their legs and quack, and the followers would be astounded to see them dance to the tunes of the guru.

Once, on Guru Purnima Day, a journalist was attending a special discourse at the ashram. There were thousands of people present, and arrangements had been made accordingly. The event was being telecast live.

Kikar Guru sat on a stage erected for the purpose, but the journalist could barely see him amid the huge crowd. He approached some disciples and asked to be allowed to sit closer to the stage. They asked him if he would like to meet the godman on the stage. 'However, only disabled people are permitted by the guru to approach him on the stage. In case you went with us on a stretcher, you could get the guru's blessings in person,' explained a disciple.

The curious journalist immediately agreed. He was taken on a stretcher to the stage and straight to the smiling Kikar Guru. As thousands of people watched in the audience, and many more through the television channels, the godman offered the journalist some prasad that he seemed to get out of nowhere, and went on to press the man's legs, that the guru had announced as paralysed. The journalist was shocked as he couldn't move. He himself had pretended to be paralysed.

The guru now asked him to step down and walk. The

journalist expressed his inability to do so. He pleaded with the guru to let him go. He was caught in his own bluff. The guru was adamant that he do as he was told. Two disciples came forward to help, so the journalist had no choice but to sit on the stretcher, put his feet down and walk on the stage. The public went wild with the *chamatkar* (miracle) they had just witnessed. Their saint had just blessed a disabled man who was cured. The inspector had the incident recorded by the media person.

Kikar Guru had more than a hundred women disciples who lived in the ashram. The inspector had always wondered why the number of women was greater than the number of men. He discovered the reason soon enough. Whenever celebrities or well-known people visited the ashram, the women there, just a few minutes before the arrival of the VIPs, would form a long queue outside the meeting hall of the guru.

On some pretext or other, they would let the visiting dignitaries know that they had been standing in lines, waiting for the past two days, and that it was quite a normal waiting time to receive darshan from the famous Kikar Guru. The celebrities would be taken to the guru through a back entrance, and they would be much impressed by the popularity of the Guru, the usual waiting period and the favour extended to the VIPs. They would listen to the godman and leave behind a thick packet of currency notes. After they left, the ashramites would disperse. The police team recorded the façade created to dupe dignified and elite followers.

In the dead of night, the guru would quietly go to the outer field of the ashram with a child, leaving footprints on the muddy path. In the morning, he would claim that he had danced with Lord Ganesh in his dream. His close disciples would then pretend to discover the footprints on the exact same path where he claimed he had danced. The other disciples, as well as visitors to the ashram, were then told about this miracle. The footprints were shown as belonging to the child avatar of Lord Ganesh. The police team was furious when they followed the guru one night and found him on the muddy path with the small boy, the son of one of his disciples. They would love to have arrested him on the spot.

The inspector found out that during a trip to another village, the guru had travelled with at least three hundred men, women and children. Midway, some disciples were tired, and they requested the guru to rest near the banks of a river. At first, the guru was reluctant, but on their repeated requests, he relented and allowed the cavalcade to halt at a particular place.

As everyone stepped out of their vehicles, a carpet was laid on a small mound near the river for the guru. He sat there sipping his tea when a disciple asked a fresh entrant to the ashram, to ask the guru for a gift. The woman, a foreigner, approached the guru and begged him to bestow any gift on her. He readily obliged and in front of three hundred disciples, started hitting the ground with his hand near where he sat. He then asked two of his disciples to carefully dig the specific spot.

To the amazement of the gathering, a beautiful idol emerged at a depth of three and a half feet. It was an antique piece depicting the dancing Lord Shiva. The woman fell to his feet, and the crowd clapped in ecstasy. In their eyes, the guru was the epitome of divinity itself.

Now, the insider who related the incident to the inspector, believing him to be another disciple, also disclosed that the entire episode had in fact been a planned one. The guru and his coterie of disciples had meticulously prearranged every step on the way. His followers feared God, and to them, the guru was their closest contact to that God. So getting them to believe that it was all an act was an impossible task.

The guru fed his followers with some fantastic stories. One such story narration happened to be in front of the police team. He told them about a time when he had been travelling on foot through a deep forest with difficult terrain. He had lost his way and had been wandering for many hours without food or water.

Suddenly, from nowhere, a beautiful child who resembled Lord Krishna appeared. The child gave him some food and water and led him towards the main path. Once back on track, the guru asked him if he was Lord Krishna himself. The child simply smiled and disappeared into thin air. At the ashram, the crowd cheered and applauded the guru's story.

The inspector, along with Ramhet, had enough material against Kikar Guru, and he decided it was time to leave. Just the day before the three men were to leave the ashram, yet another interesting incident occurred. The guru asked a rich industrialist follower to gift him a Mercedes Benz. The industrialist was reimbursed in cash by the guru. The gift documents were displayed at the entrance to the ashram, and it was announced that the Guru had been given such an expensive gift by the industrialist, who supposedly had gained much wealth, all because of his blessings.

Inspector Mohan submitted a detailed report, along with video and audio recordings, as evidence of the deceitful activities of Kikar Guru. The laboratory tests done on the vibhuti revealed that it contained a mixture of paracetamol, tobacco, perfume, menthol and MSG. The blessings were nothing but a sugarcoated Nimesulide salt with a painkiller that would give instant relief to the consumer from any pain. The tobacco and perfume intoxicated them.

The poor followers, who were relieved from their pain, would thank the guru for his super-healing powers. Further, it was found that coconuts caught fire because of the chemical reaction of glycerine that was injected into them. In addition, the fruit kernels moved on their own because there was a mouse inside them.

The police and CBI personnel swooped down on the ashram and arrested Kikar Guru on the basis of this irrefutable evidence. They also had to summon income tax sleuths, because the inner chamber of the ashram revealed more than twenty-five crore rupees in cash.

The Tax Department revealed that the godman had obtained exemption certificates in the name of the donations made to the ashram, to free himself of tax dues. He was also amassing huge wealth by charging a one-third commission to his rich disciples for converting black money into white.

The Kikar Guru and his inner circle of associates were booked under various charges, including cruelty to animals, and were sentenced to a total of twenty years of rigorous imprisonment. The news of his arrest was made public through media coverage and became extremely sensational. There were protests in the Sawai Madhopur District and other parts of Rajasthan, but the police were ready for any such eventuality. They faced the public and tried to educate the devotees about how their guru had been duping them and how godmen such as the guru thrive in our country because they are blindly worshipped by millions of people.

The ashram complex was handed over to a non-government organization to conduct programmes for the empowerment of the villagers. The site of the earlier ashram now became a symbol of liberation and prosperity for the local people. The kikar tree became a significant landmark because of the story that was attached to it.

Tourists who visited the National Park were also told of the tale of the kikar tree. As for Ramhet Meena, he was not only awarded prize money for his bravery and felicitated for helping the police nab Kikar Guru, but was also declared a hero for displaying exemplary courage in outwitting a Ranthambore tiger and saving his life.

Agnates and Cognates

It's the story of the infighting, which went about between two factions 'Agnates and Cognates'. In legal parlance, agnates mean the Class II legal heirs of a deceased who had no Class I heirs. The children of his brother(s) are known as agnates. In case such a person, who has no legal heir of his own and has only sisters, dies, the children of his sisters are known as cognates.

It is a story of a rich bachelor, a matinee idol who dies intestate, i.e., without leaving a will, and his agnates and cognates fight a violent court battle for the inheritance of his properties worth several thousand crores.

A reputed film production company has shown interest in making a film based on this intriguing story. The resemblance, if any, to some of the stars of Bollywood is incidental, and the story is purely a work of fiction.

Kumar—a matinee idol of the yesteryears and former heartthrob of millions—lay on a bed at the Breach Candy Hospital in Mumbai, waiting for the inevitable to happen. In spite of being administered life-saving drugs, his vital organs had begun to collapse. It was tragic to witness him on his deathbed, when he had spent most of the ninety years of his life in the limelight. His life had been nothing less than a dream run.

Very few people achieved so much wealth, fame and acclaim in their lifetime.

Realizing that his end was near, he sighed and murmured to himself, 'Will I ever see him again?' No! It was too late, he thought to himself. He shrugged his shoulders in despair. No one told him that he had only a few days to live, but he could read it in the expressions of the doctors, the nurses, his relatives and friends. They came to him in turns, gradually accepting the truth that in the end, death prevails and does not show mercy even to a superstar like him. They loved him for being a great artist and a good human being. He was known to ask for forgiveness for making even the slightest error. According to him, a perfect apology had three parts—'I am sorry', 'It is my fault' and 'What can I do to make it right?' The directors of his movies appreciated that despite acquiring a position where he could get away with saying or doing anything, he remained humble at heart.

The star had been under heavy sedation for a week. Nevertheless, in those last moments, many cherished memories of his life unfolded in his mind's eye like a film-reel playing on a screen in one of his theatres. His thoughts went back to the winter of 1951 when, in the dead of night, he had stealthily stolen four gold bangles—for all his mother had was a *mangalsutra* and a few bangles—and ₹2,500 rupees in cash from his mother's wooden chest. His father, a poor farmer from the village of Sirhind in Punjab, had been forced to sell two acres of agricultural land to pay off a part of his never-ending debt. Before any further payment of loan was made, Kumar decided to run off with the cash and jewellery to pursue his dream. He planned to go to Bombay (now Mumbai) to try his luck in the film industry.

Mahendrajit Singh Malik alias Kumar was an extremely handsome, tall and ambitious young lad. His performance in academics was average, but he was an ace hockey player and excelled in volleyball. It was because of his personality, charm and good looks that he was always given the hero's role to enact in the plays staged during his school and college days. In addition to his physical attributes, he was a true artist. While in college, he had the privilege of sitting with the professor in charge of the drama club and making improvements in the script, especially his dialogues. Above all, he was a natural on stage, going into a trance, truly embodying the character he portrayed. People in Sirhind referred to him as a hero. The name given by his friends and relatives had such an impact on the youngster that he decided to run away and go to Bombay to actually become a Bollywood hero.

This was at a time when the movie industry had taken the country by storm. Daily, almost a hundred people from all over India alighted at Bombay Central Station to try their luck in Bollywood. How far those youngsters were able to give wings to their aspirations was another matter. Most did not make it. Some returned to their respective cities while others took up menial jobs in Bombay with the hope that someday, Lady Luck would favour them. On 20 December 1951, Malik, too, got off a train with great hope in his heart, dreaming of becoming a part of the film industry. Just two days before, on the 18th of December, he had celebrated his twenty-sixth birthday with his relatives and friends. He had silently bid them farewell, as he was soon to leave them behind in Sirhind to fulfil his dream.

His journey from Sirhind to Bombay was uneventful. On reaching Bombay Central Station, the first thing he did was hire a Victoria carriage to take him to the nearest place to catch a view of the Arabian Sea for the first time in his life. In the days that followed his arrival, an endless struggle of routinely visiting studios, directors and producers from Bombay to Pune, tested his patience. It was all to no avail. In spite of his good looks and athletic physique, he was shown the door at every studio. He understood that it was not going to be easy to enter the industry without continued perseverance or a godfather.

A year passed. Malik had neither written a letter nor tried to call up the Sirhind post office to inform his parents of his whereabouts. He had begun to feel depressed, working as a waiter in the canteen of a film studio. After spending all the money he had stolen from his home, he had even sold his mother's gold bangles. Almost penniless, Malik was seriously contemplating heading back to his hometown when he was noticed by a renowned actress at the studio canteen.

She recommended him to one of her producers, who gave him a small role in his upcoming film and appointed him as an employee in his film company at a salary of ₹150 per month. Malik began to do all kinds of small jobs for the producer—on the production floor as well as side roles in the latter's movies, whenever the opportunity arose. As luck would have it, the audience as well as the film fraternity noticed him in a small role and, subsequently, his life took a turn for the better. He first became a supporting actor, and then quickly graduated to becoming a lead actor in film after film. The actress who had recommended him was in time paired with him, and their onscreen chemistry was loved by the audience. Mahendrajit Singh Malik was renamed Kumar by one of the most successful producers and directors of the 1960s. He resigned from the film production company and began to independently sign on to movies in his new avatar. His films were released one after another, and in the span of three years, he became very popular and well sought-after.

Kumar was happy with the way things had turned out for him. He had been able to establish himself in his dream profession and was sure that his future was bright. He drew the courage to contact his parents back home. He not only asked their forgiveness and reassured them of his well-being, but also sent them money to support them.

He went on to deliver several successful, acting performances during the 1960s and was admired and loved by audiences all over the country. As a gifted actor, he could play a diverse range of characters with effortless ease. Be it a romantic role or a tragic one, he was credited with bringing realism to film acting. After an acting career spread out over ten years, critics lauded him as one of the greatest actors in the history of Indian cinema.

By 1967, he had acted in more than thirty films and had won a Filmfare Award for Best Actor and a National Award for an offbeat film. He was a sensational performer and was often compared to Hollywood actors of his time. In fact, his popularity brought him an offer for a role in a Hollywood film. Eager to experiment, he soon left for Los Angeles, spending the next six months there, shooting for his film and enjoying the Hollywood life. He was enamoured with the affluent lifestyle of the actors there, including their spectacular villas and classy convertibles.

Kumar returned to Bombay after the shoot and resumed his work in Bollywood. He purchased a sprawling bungalow in Juhu and brought his entire family from Punjab—his parents, his elder sister and two younger brothers who were now married, and their families—to live with him. His bungalow had eleven rooms, and an annexe was constructed to accommodate a gym and some sports facilities. He spent money on them and made sure that his family members were very comfortably settled in. He believed it was one way of making up for his actions in the past. After he had run away with the cash and jewellery, a gloom had descended upon his family. His father had vowed never to see his face again, but all of that was in the past—forgiven and forgotten. The family began living a happy life in Bombay while Kumar delivered successful film performances, one after the other. He earned huge amounts of money and started accumulating assets.

In a place like Bombay, a person understood the power of money very quickly. Even Kumar realized this, although a little late. He came from a small city, where everyone was willing to make sacrifices for others without thinking about personal gains. In Bombay, the harsh reality was that only money mattered. Here, everyone battled for survival, and only the shrewd and the cunning won. Simpletons lost money to fraudsters. At first, Kumar, too, lay his trust in the wrong people. He believed their words to be sincere and well-meaning and was cheated by those who proclaimed to be his friends. However, over time, he became wiser, investing his substantial earnings in purchasing properties all over India. He became wealthier than any other actor before him did. Money poured in from everywhere. His careful investments began yielding him rich dividends. In the coming decades, Kumar hired his team of managers to look after his real estate interest.

During the remake of a hit Telugu film in Hindi, in lieu of money, Kumar requested the producer to transfer one of the latter's commercial properties located at the outskirts of the city to him as his professional fee if the film became a success. It did. The producer happily handed over the possession of the entire commercial complex to Kumar. Over time, the city located in South India spread out, and the property on the outskirts became a central part of it. Kumar, along with some of his associates, demolished the commercial area and converted it into the first mall complex of the city. It was named Kumar Capital Mall, and he let out the entire complex at a hefty monthly rent of several lakhs of rupees. His wealth continued to grow by leaps and bounds and the rentals received were wisely reinvested in properties.

Kumar had love affairs with many of his leading ladies, but he never married any of them. He was very generous and supportive of social causes, actively donating money to various charitable organizations. He often inaugurated the shops and offices of his associates without charging a single rupee or demanding any favour in return.

When Kumar was sixty-two, he tried his hand at making a film. The theme was based on his own experiences, and he relied upon his instincts rather than mainstream formulas to make the film. From scriptwriting to painstakingly selecting the cast and crew, Kumar was deeply involved in the direction and production of the movie.

When the movie was completed and shown to the distributors, nobody was willing to take it up. The film was about him struggling to make a mark but failing miserably and dying in the end. The distributors said nothing, but when the screening was over, it was written large on their faces that they were not in line with Kumar's concept and his debut directorial effort. People criticized it and the critics rejected the theme of the film for depicting adultery. It was objectionable, according to the provisions of the Cinematograph Act. The Censor Board received anonymous letters advocating a ban on the film from public exhibition. The film did not receive an 'A' certificate.

Kumar approached the Minister of Information and Broadcasting with a request to view the film and the minister agreed to do so. Kumar brought the reels of the movie to Delhi from Bombay, and a private screening was carried out before the minister. He was taking a chance, but it turned out to be a prudent move on Kumar's part. After the movie had been screened, the minister agreed to grant clearance if a few scenes were deleted, changed and re-shot. Kumar readily agreed.

The film was released pan India with a lot of publicity, but initially, audiences were quite confused by it. The picture was so intense that it left them completely stunned. As the weeks went by, no word of appreciation came from any corner. The superstar was puzzled. It was turning out to be a disaster.

It was in the second month of its release that the film picked up, and people began discussing it. It went on to become the highest-grossing Bollywood film of the century. The movie was declared an all-time classic and won almost every major film fraternity award. Cash flowed in. Kumar came out victorious in his debut production and directorial venture.

Years later, Kumar received an invitation from the chief minister of Punjab to inaugurate a charitable multispecialty hospital named after him. Kumar was overwhelmed by the prospect of setting foot once again on the soil of Sirhind—the place that he had formerly belonged to. He felt a deep pang in his heart that his parents and close relatives would not be present to share the jubilation of his visit as a state guest—an honour bestowed upon him by the chief minister himself.

Thousands of people had gathered to welcome their superstar in Sirhind. When Kumar visited his childhood home, he wept bitterly at the sight of his old, dilapidated house. The sound and smell of his home, the faces of his family members, the memories of his mother cooking for him as she wiped the sweat from her brow, it all came back to him, and Kumar felt like a child once again.

The natives of Sirhind applauded his emotional speech with a sense of pride. Kumar also met his close friends from the past who had remained in the town and did various jobs. They were there to welcome him. He presented them with expensive gifts that they happily accepted. After spending three days in Sirhind, he went back to Bombay with a heavy heart. He donated a cheque of one crore rupees from his personal account for the development of his hometown.

By the end of the twentieth century, Kumar—the doyen of the Hindi film industry as he had come to be known—had become the richest film star of his time and was paying a huge amount of wealth and income tax to government authorities. His honesty and loyalty towards the country were beyond the comprehension of the film fraternity, which mostly depended on undisclosed funds. In his later years, he continued to act in films, having changed to character roles and kept himself busy doing television advertisements.

As the years passed by and old age caught up, Kumar preferred to spend most of his time at home. It was while celebrating his eighty-sixth birthday in 2011, that he realized how alone he was. By that time, his parents, brothers and their wives, and his sister and her husband had all passed away, leaving only his nieces and nephews with him. While his brothers had four children—all daughters, his sister had three sons. He loved them as if they were his own children. Some of them had shifted to apartments owned by him in Colaba and Marine Drive in Bombay, or Mumbai—as the city was renamed. Kumar's nieces and nephews lived on his wealth and were the caretakers of his vast empire. Their sole occupation was to look after his properties, rental earnings and theatres spread across India. Even the four sons-in-law were involved in managing his estates. All of them reported the financial status of his vast properties and businesses on a monthly basis to the star. One day, Kumar was informed that they were siphoning off funds and mismanaging his earnings. He did not pay heed to his auditors' advice of curbing misappropriation and unaccounted expenditure. He brushed aside the warnings because they were his family, his support system.

Moreover, they helped him manage his assets, and he believed that he had enough wealth to bear small misappropriations. As long as the bottom line showed profits, he was not alarmed. He was still the highest taxpayer of the film fraternity.

Kumar summoned his lawyer and friend, Ramesh Deshmukh to draw up his will. In the current situation, with his brothers and sisters having passed on, he wished to distribute his assets among his nephews and nieces, who were now his legal heirs.

His lawyer explained to him that in the absence of any immediate blood relation—since Kumar had not married and did not have any children—it meant that he had no Class I legal heir. He only had Agnates and Cognates. Hearing such legal jargon for the first time, Kumar looked at Ramesh in bewilderment. The lawyer explained to him that according to The Hindu Succession Act of 1956, after his demise, his properties would endow upon his two younger brothers' children (agnates) and in case, the agnates were not alive, to his sister's children (cognates). This would happen if he died without leaving a will. In case he executed a will, his wealth would be endowed as per the contents of his will and then the Succession Act to agnates and cognates would not be applicable, only what was written in the registered will would be bequeathed to his legal heirs. The lawyer also advised that the will should be duly registered and videotaped, leaving no chance for any legal heir to challenge it later.

It was Kumar's ninetieth birthday. Like always, he was preparing to celebrate the day when he was visited by officers from the Income Tax department. The Income Tax department had decided to level allegations of earning unaccounted money against Kumar, something for which the film industry was notorious. The appraisal report prepared by the officers not only suggested the imposition of fine and penalties on him, but recommended prosecution for the evasion of taxes.

Firstly, the Income Tax department had received information that there was, on a massive scale, siphoning of funds within the firms and companies run by his relatives. Secondly, the department officials had recently conducted an income tax raid on a film producer, and a journal had been found in the latter's possession, giving explicit details of massive amounts in cash having been paid to Kumar by the producer. Kumar had no idea about both the cases, but it was damning evidence for the officers and the department seized the invoices from his premises.

When the vigilance department made inquiries, they found that the bills were all fake as the companies whose names were present on the invoices did not exist. This made matters extremely difficult for Kumar. Even if his relatives were running the businesses on his behalf, he was accountable for their actions and wrongdoings because he was the owner of all the companies. He consulted his lawyers and chartered accountants and realized that if he put the blame on his relatives, he would have to face the legal consequences, according to the provisions of The Benami

Transactions (Prohibition) Act, 1988. Kumar did not give up. Even if he was not at fault personally, he decided to fight the case. He also decided to pay his taxes and revise his returns.

In the case of the fictitious bills, he surrendered huge amounts of money and paid taxes. However, he got relief from the tax tribunal on the payments shown in the diary of the producer. Kumar's lawyers shrewdly confronted and questioned the producer before the tax authorities. They asked the producer to narrate the details of the transactions and give the names of the witnesses in front of whom the payments were made. The producer fumbled and ultimately revealed the truth. He had withdrawn the money from the bank for himself, but for accounting purposes, he had entered transactions in the name of Kumar, in connivance with the latter's nephews.

Kumar was extremely disturbed by the events that had taken place. He remembered being warned about the misappropriations taking place behind his back and his auditors' advice to take cautionary measures to check the actions of his family members. He summoned Ramesh Deshmukh once again to make immediate changes in the contents of his will. Deshmukh, over the years, had grown to be more than just a lawyer to Kumar. He had become a close confidante and was like a brother to him. According to Kumar's instructions, the lawyer drafted a final will to supersede the earlier one. However, as circumstances would have it, Kumar suffered a heart stroke before the newly drafted will could be signed and now lay hospitalized.

The signing of the will was kept on hold. The doctors informed Kumar's close relatives regarding the inevitable. Kumar had only a few days.

Kumar's agnates and cognates pretended to show their respects to him. In reality, they wished for his demise so that they could distribute his assets and become legal owners of their share.

During his brief moments of consciousness, Kumar was given details of the activities outside the hospital. Ramesh Deshmukh told him that his relatives were fighting amongst themselves. The four daughters of his brothers, along with their husbands, had drawn swords against his sister's three sons. They blamed each other for the money that had been siphoned from the companies. There were rumours that Kumar had prepared a new will and his relatives were petrified that they would be ousted from it.

Kumar was utterly disgruntled at this unfortunate turn of events. He could never have imagined that he would live to see his heirs stoop to such lows and make enemies out of each other. All this while, his health was steadily deteriorating.

But Kumar also remembered those good times that he had never shared with anyone. He remembered the time spent in America. He thought of the beautiful Maria, the love of his life, whom he had met forty years ago in America. Being as famous as he was, he had been very careful with keeping his identity unknown. He wished to keep his privacy. He had vowed to carry this secret love affair with him to his grave, except for Ramesh Deshmukh. His friend was the only person who knew that side of him. Kumar remembered the good times he had spent with Maria in New York and Los Angeles, and the memory of her warmed his otherwise desolate heart, as he lay in the hospital.

He came back to reality for the last time when his eldest niece touched his hand affectionately. He smiled at her with effort and looked at his agnates and cognates, who had gathered there to see their benefactor. Soon after, his lungs gave way, and he had to be put on a ventilator. He never regained consciousness.

Media reporters waiting outside the hospital, who had been reporting the status of Kumar's failing health 24/7, now spread the news of his death. The information spread like wildfire, and a large crowd gathered outside Breach Candy Hospital.

The funeral procession included eminent film personalities and dignitaries among the thousands of fans, all wanting to pay homage to their departed superstar. The agnates and cognates, hostile as they had become towards each other, began an argument among themselves while selecting the relative who would light the pyre and perform the last rites. Well-wishers intervened and were somehow able to resolve the issue by asking the oldest nephew, Kamaljit, to perform the rites. But the nephews and husbands of the nieces continued to jostle each other, each trying to gain a better position in view of the media cameras. A fight nearly broke out when the oldest niece's husband, Narendrajit, held Kamaljit's hand, stopping him from lighting the funeral pyre. The elders present, including Ramesh Deshmukh, resolved the matter by having both of them conduct the ritual together.

True to character, Kumar surprised his fans and relatives after his demise. On the fourth day after his death, a ceremony was performed at the Wankhede Stadium in Mumbai, attended by almost twenty thousand people. A video recording of Kumar taken years back was played on huge screens. That was the Kumar that he had wanted his fans and all loved ones to remember him by as—the one who had been full of life and had lived on his own terms. In his speech, he thanked the gathering for attending his death ceremony and expressed his gratitude to all his producers, co-stars, relatives and friends, who had been his pillars of strength throughout his life. He thanked millions of fans who had supported him, from all over the world. The speech ended with an Urdu couplet from one of his famous films, leaving the crowd in tears, cheering and applauding the legend.

On the thirteenth day after Kumar's demise, Ramesh Deshmukh read out the actor's unsigned will in front of all of his agnates and cognates. Kumar had bequeathed a part of his wealth to them. The will also stated that the details regarding the distribution of his remaining wealth would be revealed at a later date. Silence prevailed for a long time. The agnates and cognates looked at each other in confusion. They tried to argue with the lawyer and threatened to challenge the will.

Kumar's heirs issued legal notices against each other, questioning the validity of the unsigned will. The cognates were led by Kamaljit, while the agnates were led by Narendrajit. The cognates believed that they had been given a raw deal. They said that compared to the agnates, they had been given less value in terms of Kumar's wealth and wanted equal distribution of the assets and properties. The agnates, on the other hand, challenged the legality of the unsigned and unregistered will. They petitioned the court to invoke The Hindu Succession Act of 1956, stating that in the absence of any Class I legal heir, they were entitled to the assets owned by the film star. Legal battles in the High Court of Mumbai ensued and the judges, after hearing the arguments of the lawyers, ordered status quo to be maintained till the final decision about the will was made.

The squabbling among the legal heirs of Kumar soon reached its pinnacle. Kamaljit looked after two huge farmhouses in Khandala near Mumbai that was valued at three hundred crore rupees. Narendrajit, taking several of his men along with him, tried to wrest possession of the farmhouses. They pelted stones and used sticks to beat up the security. Both parties fought with each other. There were injuries on both sides. In spite of the assault, Narendrajit could not gain possession of the farmhouses. But the act of physical assault crossed all boundaries of decency between the feuding relatives.

The agnates and cognates had long meetings with their lawyers. Numerous cases were filed, which only served to escalate the situation. Employees-turned-informants were paid hefty sums for providing information about their respective bosses' next move. Some gave false information to the other side for easy money, while some employees gave details that led to bitter confrontations between the two camps. The agnates and cognates had declared war against each other.

The situation affected the majority of Kumar's companies adversely. Businesses suffered, work was suspended, theatres shut down and chaos prevailed. Huge amount of money was spent by both parties in trying to win over corrupt government officers to their side. The family's legal battles resulted in properties being eventually handed over to a custodian appointed by the court. However, before the custodian could act on the high court's orders, an application was filed by a John Witkins at the Mumbai High Court, through Ramesh Deshmukh, claiming the right to the wealth left by Kumar. The agnates and cognates received the shock of their lives when they read the contents of the petition filed by the unknown John Witkins.

Ramesh Deshmukh was proceeding according to special instructions given to him by Kumar before the latter's death. He proceeded to stage the dramatic entry of John Witkins in the court. The lawyer, while presenting the petition, sought permission from the judge to present the star, Kumar himself, to the court. The shocked prosecutor asked him if he was out of his mind. How could he present someone who was no longer alive? The judge too had a perplexed expression, and reprimanded the lawyer, asking him not to waste the court's time. But Ramesh Deshmukh requested for permission vehemently, saying he needed only a few minutes to rest the case once and for all. The judge granted him permission.

All eyes turned to the entrance as a 'Kumar' indeed entered the court, wearing a well-known outfit from one of his successful movies. People knew the outfit— it had been a sensation. They gasped. The agnates and cognates stood up, horrified at the turn of events. As the figure came forward, the judge heaved a sigh of relief and leaned back in his chair. He had attended the death ceremony of Kumar, and his shock now turned to amusement, seeing the replica of Kumar entering the courtroom in such a dramatic fashion.

John Witkins, though fairer than his father, had blonde hair that he had covered with a black wig to impersonate the esteemed star. His mannerisms, stature and build were akin to that of the late actor. The shrewd Ramesh Deshmukh disclosed to the court that the drama was essential to prove one point—that John was Kumar's son and Class I legal heir. He was Kumar's child, born out of wedlock with Maria, with whom Kumar had spent much time in America, years ago.

John Witkins stated in his affidavit that he was born of Mahendrajit Singh Malik, alias Kumar, and Maria Witkins. As evidence, he handed over his DNA report to the court. His DNA matched that of Kumar's. The evidence placed before the court left no doubt about John Witkin's claim to be Kumar's son.

Kumar had kept this part of his life a closely guarded secret. He had always cherished a desire to have children. He had fathered a child with Maria, the love of his life. Kumar, during his last days, had wanted to meet his son. The child had now grown to be a forty-year-old architect residing in New York.

John had been unaware that he was the only son and legal heir to one of the most legendary actors in Bollywood. He was informed of his true parentage by his mother a day after his father's demise, when Ramesh Deshmukh had contacted her on the instructions of Kumar. It was because of the situation between the agnates and cognates, their disloyalty to Kumar, their constant rivalry, and disgraceful actions that Kumar had felt compelled to take the drastic action of calling his son. Kumar went against his own decision to leave Maria and John out of his will, having previously settled them financially before his return to India. He had called Ramesh Deshmukh and given him the necessary instructions.

Assessing the situation to be a hopeless one, the agnates and cognates banded together against the new threat. A truce was proclaimed. They knew that they stood no chance in front of John Witkins, who was a Class I heir and the first in the line of inheritors. The court passed judgment in John Witkin's favour, and he inherited the entirety of his father's wealth.

John had realized that even though the High Court had passed the verdict in his favour, it would be tedious for him to battle the case should it go to the Supreme Court, or if he took possession of the properties that had been handled by the agnates and cognates. The nieces and nephews had been occupying those assets for years, some for almost four decades. Ramesh Deshmukh drew a Family Settlement Deed and had it signed by all the agnates and cognates, keeping the right and possession of 60 per cent of the assets to John Witkins and 20 per cent each to the agnates and cognates.

Kumar's dying wish had been to see his son before his passing, but that was not to be. If only the agnates and cognates had been grateful for the blessings they had, they would have been showered with much more. Kumar was a legend, who had changed the course of destiny by changing his mind about keeping Maria and John away from his life. He had established that he lived life on his own terms, making sure they remained unchanged even after his death.

Tiger Trail

This story is all about a vagabond orphan who became a cook at the residence of some small-time animal skin smugglers. The shrewd orphan later becomes one of the biggest tiger skin smugglers—a ruthless poacher who was feared in the country by one and all. The story is a work of fiction but inspired from a renowned poacher of North India. The notorious poacher faced charges for allegedly selling 470 tigers, 2,130 leopards and several thousand snake skins. The story is made into a film which conveys a strong message about putting an end to poaching and saving the endangered species.

Based on this story, a film has been made by SR Series production. The story and screenplay of the film Tiger Trail *have been written by the authors of this book. It stars actors of repute such as Dharmendra, Rati Agnihotri, Annu Kapoor, Kamaal Khan, Raju Srivastava, etc., in stellar roles. It portrays Suresh K. Raheja and the author Sunil Kapoor, too, in meaty roles.*

Tiger Trail *is an endeavour to save tigers by the renowned animal lover Suresh K. Raheja who has composed music and sang a few songs in the film, too. Sunil Kapoor has debuted as a singer in this film.*

A yellow and black-striped Royal Bengal Tiger, also called the Indian tiger, roamed in the dense forest of a national park near the town of Ramnagar that is situated in the Nainital district of the state of Uttarakhand. It moved in a leisurely manner and its skin shone a yellow-orange with the rays of the sun that fell directly on it. It walked majestically towards a bank of River Kosi to quench its thirst. Tigers, belonging to the class of Panthera Tigris, are one of the largest cat species and most valuable, being an endangered lot. But this one was oblivious to the more dangerous species—human poachers. Shamsher Singh Rana, lurking not far behind, was a notorious killer of tigers. He moved stealthily in the direction of the tiger, following the footprints of the glorious beast.

Shamsher was a henchman of the infamous Lohar Chand—the dreaded poacher known to smuggle hundreds of animal skins to China and Europe. Lohar Chand rewarded his protégés handsomely for the skins brought to him, but he was ruthless too and sent those who dared to betray him to their deaths.

A monkey screeched, signalling the arrival of the tiger to the other animals. Shamsher gestured to his four comrades wearing military uniforms and bearing guns—who followed at a close distance—to maintain silence as they moved towards the river bank after their prey.

Shamsher turned a bend and saw his prey fifty yards away, drinking from the river with its front paws submerged into the river. He smiled and raised his .303 rifle, but before he could take aim at the animal, an alligator suddenly emerged from the water and opened its jaws. The tiger backed away from the alligator's reach and moved to a safe distance. Shamsher and his men followed for the kill. This was not going to be an easy task, he thought, as he raised his rifle again. Sensing activity, the tiger turned towards where the men were hiding. Shamsher was in luck, and he fired. Before the tiger could react, a bullet pierced its skull, and the royal beast fell instantly. Shamsher was quick to act. He fired two more shots to ward off the alligator and forced it to swim towards deeper water, away from the bank. The gunfire also served as a warning for other animals to keep away. Shamsher instructed his men to bring the equipment from their jeep to carry the tiger's body. After loading their kill, they drove from Jim Corbett National Park towards their hideout in the outskirts of Ramnagar.

Lohar Chand was pleased to see one more dead tiger brought to his storehouse. He counted the total number of animal skins in his possession. There were twenty-six tiger skins, thirty-four leopard skins and 200 snake skins—all worth a few crores in rupees.

Lohar Chand's real name was Laxmi Chand. He had been brought up in an orphanage in Maharashtra. He had been through a lot of traumatic experiences in his childhood. He was often beaten up by Jeevan, the unscrupulous and cruel caretaker of the orphanage who derived pleasure in thrashing children at the smallest pretext. The poor children of the orphanage begged him not to hit them, but he never spared anyone. They were scared of the caretaker and so complied with all his instructions regarding the daily chores. They cleaned all three floors of the building, did laundry, cooked meals and in return, got a regular thrashing. Jeevan pocketed the money the orphanage was given as government funding instead of paying for servants. He sold the rations supposedly given for the orphans and also peddled small handicraft items made by the children.

Laxmi Chand was the most notorious of all the orphans

in the establishment and was thrashed the most by Jeevan. He was always up to mischief. Bunty, another orphan, was the best behaved amongst them, often taking the blame for Laxmi's wrongdoings and receiving punishment for them. Older than Laxmi by two years, Bunty wanted to get the latter on the path of righteousness, but Laxmi was an angry teenager who hated the wily Jeevan, and so, often misbehaved.

As time went by, Bunty and Laxmi had grown tall and strong for their age. Bunty was unaware of the hatred the other had amassed for Jeevan. When Laxmi was thirteen years old, he was unable to take it anymore and finally had his revenge. One day, when the old Jeevan was beating the boys, Laxmi snatched the stick from Jeevan and hit him in retaliation. Bunty leapt forward and held Laxmi's hand, but the damage was done. Laxmi had given two lethal blows to Jeevan's head. Blood oozed from the caretaker's bald head, and he fell to the ground, unconscious. Laxmi panicked and ran from the orphanage.

Bunty ran after him to catch him and return to the orphanage. Laxmi ran fast, wanting to get as far away as possible from the scene of his crime. There was a railway line a couple of kilometres away, and while crossing it, he saw a train slowing down. Without thinking, he boarded the moving train. Bunty did the same. They did not have enough money on them to buy tickets and managed to not get caught by the ticket collector. In an hour, the train reached Mumbai. Bunty wanted to return to the orphanage along with Laxmi immediately and called up the orphanage, only to be told that the caretaker had succumbed to his injuries and had died at the hospital. Bunty was scared and confused, but Laxmi had no regrets. He felt a very strange power surging through him after committing his first murder. He, thereafter, vowed to kill anyone who tried to lay their hands on him. His only regret was not having put an end to Jeevan earlier.

In the days that followed, the boys followed their natural instincts. When he felt the pangs of extreme hunger, Laxmi would steal food from shops. Bunty would refuse to eat stolen food and Laxmi would eat it all. Soon, Bunty took up employment as a utility worker in a small restaurant in Colaba, and Laxmi disappeared into the slums of Dharavi.

The police recorded Laxmi's name as a murderer and Bunty's as an absconder from the orphanage. The juvenile court passed an ex parte order against Laxmi for committing a heinous crime. The police were now on a lookout for him and Bunty.

Destiny led Laxmi to a smuggler's house where he got the job of cleaning the floors and washing the dishes. Laxmi was hardworking and had a sharp mind. He soon realized that his employers were dealing in the covert purchase and sale of animal skins. He started doing small but risky jobs for his employers and made extra money by involving himself in petty criminal activities.

At the age of fifteen, he was already a part of various small gangs operating from the slums of Dharavi and was willing to do any kind of job. He was strong, stout and brazen, and prudently followed all the instructions of his gangster employer. Gradually, he learned the finer points of the business of smuggling animal skins and built his connections in the underworld. He began his own independent trade of animal skins without the knowledge of his masters. With his first major earning, he bought a revolver.

By the time Laxmi was eighteen, he had a small gang of his own and was dealing in the skins of snakes, rabbits, fox and deer. His notoriety became well known, and he was infamous in the slums of Dharavi. His activities were not hidden anymore, and his employers learned of his independent poaching trade through their contacts. This infuriated them, and they confronted him. The argument led to a heated scuffle, and in a three-to-one fight, Laxmi was badly beaten. Infuriated, he took out his revolver and impulsively shot his employer, who died on the spot. Now the Dharavi gangsters, as well as the police, were after Laxmi. He escaped to the nearby Koyna Wild Sanctuary and hid in the jungles there. He killed animals to satisfy his hunger and was careful never to leave any trace that could be tracked by forest officers. He was not afraid of the darkness or living alone in a dense forest.

After three months of living in the jungles, Laxmi made his way back to his house in Dharavi. That night, he quietly dug out the savings that he had hidden in the form of cash and gold biscuits. He met his gang, and after laying out a plan for them to meet him in secrecy, he left for the Koyna jungles. With money at his disposal, he bought long-range rifles and ammunition. Soon his gang joined him, and they were back in business.

Now that Laxmi understood the trade inside out, he eliminated the need for hiring hunters and middlemen. The gang did all the work themselves. They killed animals and sold the skins directly to buyers, thereby making huge profits. Soon, the forest officers caught onto the presence of his gang operating in the area. But Laxmi was as cunning as a fox, and he wandered in the jungles from one hideout to another. When it became dangerous for him to operate in the forests of Maharashtra, he shifted to the forests of Uttarakhand and changed his name to Lohar Chand. He came to be known as the 'Poaching King'. It was a name to be dreaded in the Uttarakhand area.

While Laxmi chose the path of crime, Bunty chose the path

of honesty and hard work. Some sailors who regularly visited the restaurant in Colaba where he worked, liked his honesty and demeanour, and they offered him a job on a merchant ship. Later, Bunty joined a cruise-liner making trips from Mumbai to Goa as a utility worker.

Once, while cleaning a deck, Bunty noticed a small child leaning over the railings. Before he could call out in warning, the child lost his balance and fell into the Arabian Sea. The ship was about 15 nautical miles from the port of Vasco da Gama, Goa. Without batting an eyelid, Bunty shouted for help and jumped into the sea to rescue the child. He could see the five-year old struggling to stay afloat. He swam with all his strength and reached the child. Calming him as best as he could, Bunty hauled the child onto his back and started swimming in the direction of the ship. Members of the security staff who had heard Bunty's scream for help and had seen him jump into the sea, immediately alerted the captain. Within minutes, the engines of the liner were stopped, and a rescue operation was launched. Two lifeboats with guards were lowered into the sea.

Bunty could see the boats as he kept swimming with the child, but his hopes of survival were dashed when he saw a shark swimming towards him. As the shark drew closer, Bunty knew he faced imminent death in the jaws of the fish. He was more concerned about the little boy he was trying to save and continued to swim towards the ship as fast as he could, knowing fully well that he could not beat the shark.

Suddenly, a miraculous thing happened. A group of dolphins appeared from nowhere and began surrounding the shark. Upon seeing the dolphins, the shark went deep into the water and swam away. Sharks are scared of dolphins because they can kill them with their snout. There were screams and shouts on the deck of the ship as the crew and passengers who had gathered there witnessed the dangerous, chilling and strange scene between the shark, the dolphins and Bunty. The helpless relatives of the child were screaming and praying for his safety, and the crowd watched anxiously, hoping against hope that Bunty would make it to safety. As the shark disappeared and the rescue boats reached the child and his saviour, there was a loud cheer from the ship.

Bunty and the child were pulled up into a lifeboat and taken back to the liner where they received loud applause. The captain shook Bunty's hand in praise and said that he had upheld the honour of the crew. First aid was immediately provided to Bunty and the child whose name was Shivam. The doctors also attended to Shivam's mother, who had become hysterical.

Chaudhary Abhay Singh, Shivam's father, had also jumped into one of the lifeboats. He now held the crying boy in his arms, feeling relieved and grateful. He embraced Bunty and thanked him for saving his son's life.

Chaudhary Abhay Kumar came from an aristocratic background. He owned vast estates in and around Ramnagar in Uttarakhand and was an industrialist and philanthropist. He was also the chairman of a school and a college in Ramnagar that he himself had established. He was viewed as a noble, sincere and diligent man who had risen in life by dint of sheer hard work. Bunty had no inkling that his life would take a turn on that day and his heroic deed would result in turn of events. Good fortune was waiting to smile on him. He insisted that Bunty accept a sum of one lakh rupees from him for his heroic deed. With great reluctance, Bunty accepted the cash reward. When the cruise ended, Abhay Kumar's family thanked the crew and Bunty profusely. Giving Bunty his address, he also elicited a promise from him to visit the family in the immediate future.

He wished to do more for Bunty, he said.

After a month, Bunty took leave from his employers and visited Chaudhary Abhay Kumar's house in Ramnagar. He expressed his desire of completing his studies to Abhay Kumar and disclosed to him the story of his childhood and the circumstances under which he had left the orphanage. Chaudhary Abhay Kumar granted him free education and Bunty was enrolled in his college under his real name, Harshvardhan Singh. He was a bright student, keen to learn and excelled in his studies. Abhay Kumar developed an immense liking for him. He encouraged Harshvardhan to go for higher studies and attempt the civil services examination. When Harshvardhan cleared the test and was selected, Abhay Kumar, remembering the courage he had shown while saving Shivam from the jaws of certain death, advised him to opt for the IPS—the Indian Police Service. Harshvardhan became an IPS officer in the Uttarakhand cadre.

In due course of time, Lohar Chand, aka the Poaching King, ruled over the forests in the Uttarakhand region and flourished in the animal skin trade. Once, the police conducted a raid at one of his several hideouts. They found a huge pile of tiger and leopard skins, teeth and claws, as well as snake skins. Lohar Chand was arrested for wildlife trafficking, but later with the help of his highly paid lawyers, he was granted bail on account of lack of evidence. Over the years, he had developed contacts within the police and maintained good relationships with certain politicians, and all those connections came in handy for his release.

With his constant shifting from one place to the next, Lohar Chand's current hideout, coincidentally, fell at Ramnagar. He lived in the outskirts of the town and hunted animals within the Jim Corbett National Park. The people who worked under him were loyal and could be trusted blindly. Shamsher Singh Rana was one of them. He loved hunting animals. He was loyal and dependable, and Lohar Chand entrusted him with all the killings. In fact, Shamsher was the key aide in his trusted lot of people. Apart from this inner circle, Lohar Chand had around two hundred people working for him. His hunters brought him all kinds of animal skins regularly, and he rewarded them well.

Lohar Chand and his gang had become a menace, and government officials wanted to curb this menace. Shamsher Singh heard about it, and he cautioned Lohar Chand. He informed him of a meeting between the newly-appointed forest officer, the assistant commissioner of police and Chaudhary Abhay Kumar—the richest man in Ramnagar, who was also known as the "lone crusader" for the protests that he carried out against poaching. Shamsher warned his boss that he had received warnings that a Special Task Force had been set up and orders had been given to arrest the poachers. According to the government officers, Lohar Chand was a key player in the animal skin trade in North India, and his immediate arrest was essential. He had become their prime target.

Lohar Chand laughed. He boasted to his aide that nobody would dare lay their hands on him, let alone arrest him. He had high connections with politicians and police, who would protect him. He wore a cynical smile, believing that either the officers had no choice but to accept the bundle of currency notes he would send for them, or face the consequences for refusing him. It was for them to decide. Lohar Chand laughed, 'How else could I have become the kingpin without the support of corrupt government officers? Shamsher, you are too naïve. Anyone who stands in my path will not be spared. Stop worrying about me and get back into the jungles. Your work is to kill animals. I prefer dead ones to the ones alive.'

Shamsher bowed his head and was about to leave when Lohar Chand called out to him and said, 'At times, I think Veerappan follows my steps in South India and carries out his killings in my style. But I am the number one in my trade, Shamsher, no one can beat me. Tell me, is the forest officer the same Suresh Kumar, who had the brilliant idea of installing electric mannequins?'

'Yes, boss! Because of our constant attack on tigers, two of them had turned into man-eaters. Suresh Kumar installed mannequins with an electric current in various parts of the Uttarakhand forests. Whenever the man-eaters attacked the mannequins, believing them to be humans, they experienced electric shocks. Gradually, they turned back into animal predators,' Shamsher replied.

He tried to caution his master by saying that Suresh Kumar was an intelligent officer and should not be taken lightly, but he was not heard.

Bunty, aka Harshvardhan Singh, had become assistant commissioner of police (ACP) and was posted to Ramnagar. He now met his mentor, Chaudhary Abhay Kumar, along with Suresh Kumar, to discuss the plan to arrest Lohar Chand and his gang members. The ACP told him that they had received reliable information regarding Lohar Chand's whereabouts through an informer, and along with the task force, they intended to arrest the poacher and his men. They discussed their strategy and dispersed.

The Special Task Force swung into action. They spread their manpower in and around the forest area where Lohar Chand was currently operating. Barriers were installed, and groups of officers guarded their respective locations. The ACP, the forest officer and the lone crusader, along with their special teams, took to the forests and followed the tiger trails. They knew that if they trailed the tiger tracks, they would be able to catch Lohar Chand's hunters, and through those men, they would eventually apprehend Lohar Chand. And they were right. Three hunters were caught on a track, trailing a tiger. Engrossed as they were in hunting their kill, they did not realize that they were being targeted by the officers. They had no time to react and were easily overpowered. The hunters gave up when thrashed and questioned, disclosing the details of the whereabouts of Lohar Chand.

Lohar Chand was deep in the forest in his hideout, displaying his large collection to his buyers and arrogantly proclaiming that he was the most sought-after poacher in India. He boasted that he had just killed black bucks and that his men were roasting them for their dinner. Suddenly, the headlights of several jeeps startled them. ACP Harshvardhan Singh had an entire task force with him covering the hideout. Lohar Chand realized that this time, he could not escape. He was trapped. But he was not going to give up without a fight. He signalled to his men to open fire. A fight ensued. Lohar Chand tried to escape under cover of the firing but was nabbed. His buyers offered to surrender and were lined up against a wall. As he saw six of his men fall to bullets, Lohar Chand had to give in.

ACP Harshwardhan ordered the forces to ceasefire as he wanted Lohar Chand to be caught alive.

'No one can save you now, Lohar Chand,' shouted the ACP. Come out of your hideout and surrender before me. Finding himself in a tricky situation, Lohar Chand came out and dropped his weapon. Three policemen caught hold of him and brought him to the ACP.

'You can't kill me Harsh, or should I call you Bunty? We have been friends. Remember, we ran away together from the orphanage? I know everything about you, Bunty. I did not want to hurt you. Otherwise, I would have gotten you killed when you were posted here as a deputy commissioner some years back.

The ACP looked at Lohar and said, 'I knew you were tormented by the orphanage caretaker; everyone was. But, when I saw you killing Jeevan brutally, I could not believe my eyes. I could not believe that a friend of mine could do such a thing. I thought maybe it was all the anger, and that you would change with time, but you never did and have committed so many crimes that your punishment is nothing less than death by a court of law. You started poaching and killing animals because of your greed. We laid this trap for you under the instructions of the Ministry of Home Affairs. We have waited for this day, to not only arrest you but to also catch these Chinese and European smugglers red-handed. Your time is up Lohar Chand, or shall I call you Laxmi!'

He continued, 'And the informer this time was your own protégé, Shamsher Singh Rana.'

Harshvardhan Singh continued, explaining sternly where his friend had gone wrong. He said that Laxmi had chosen the wrong path, whereas he had chosen the path of truth. He pointed to Laxmi that 'cheater, liar, smuggler, and the killer of innocent animals' had become the latter's alternative name. The commissioner revealed that he had planted his men in Laxmi's group to know of his whereabouts and track him down.

'You were indeed my friend, but this uniform represents my duty for my nation. There is nothing above duty Laxmi. Chaudhary Abhay Kumar gave me the chance to live my life in the right direction. He encouraged me to study and reach a good position in my life, and here I am, standing in front of you as a commissioner of police,' concluded Harshvardhan Singh.

'Yes, yes, Bunty. But you cannot imagine the amount of wealth that I have amassed. I have so much money that in case you do not put me behind the bars and allow me to go scot-free, I will give you so much money and jewels that you have never seen in your life. I may have done wrong deeds, but people respect me and bow before my power and richness. I have travelled to various countries to sell tiger skins and earned a lot of money. What have you achieved but for a few medals? People are in awe of me,' he boasted.

'No, no, Laxmi. You are again wrong. People are in awe of you because of fear that you instil in them, wielding a pistol in your hand. You are uncouth, unscrupulous and a murderer who is a menace to not only these innocent animals but human beings too. You cannot gloat on ill-gotten wealth. I want none of it. My duty is to arrest you and the courts will do the rest,' he stated with pride.

'You will regret your decision Bunty. No judge will sentence me. I have a battery of lawyers to assist me and some judges are corrupt. Let me go Bunty. For old time's sake,' pleaded the killer on finding a determined police official.

'No, Laxmi. This time I will see that you rot in jail and if not hanged till death, are sentenced to at least lifetime imprisonment,' replied the police commissioner, showing more determination than ever.

Lohar Chand leaped forward and held a woman officer hostage, demanding that everyone drop their weapons or risk her death at his hands. But before he could say or do anything, two bullets were fired in his direction. Harshvardhan Singh had fired two shots from his revolver, instantly killing the dreaded poacher. The bullets had pierced through his skull and blood, along with a portion of grey matter oozed out from the fatal injury of the dreaded criminal.

The Special Task Force arrested the foreign smugglers and Lohar Chand's entire gang. A search of the poacher's hideouts led to the unearthing of hundreds of animal skins and other body parts, and also millions stashed in foreign and Indian currencies in lockers.

A tiger trail had put an end to the activities of the most-dreaded poacher the country had ever seen, bringing to fruition a plan that had been in the making for years.

Spark of the Divine

This story relates to the Almighty and the power that He wields. An atheist goes through numerous trials and tribulations to eventually realize that everything that happens on this planet is as per the will of God.

It's a pure work of fiction but sends a strong message to non-believers. In this story, a famous surgeon eventually understands the strength that prayers carry and the spark perpetuated by the Divine.

The will of God is supreme and no amount of arguments can dissuade a fragile woman who had immense faith in Him to pray for the impossible to happen.

The rough weather was about to take its toll. The private jetliner, a Boeing 737, owned by the world-famous Dr Sanjay Sachdev, had developed rapid depressurization due to a technical failure in one of its engines. There were only a few minutes left before it would nosedive to destruction and kill all its passengers instantly.

Dr Sanjay Sachdev had six crew members on board with him: the pilot, co-pilot, two air hostesses and two stewards. Dr Sanjay, the chairman of Medical Facilities Enterprises, was born in India. He was an excellent student of science at school and college. He migrated to America to pursue his studies and excelled in the field of medicine. At an early age, he attained a pinnacle in his profession and was considered not only one of the most successful cancer surgeons in the United States of America but also one of the richest doctors in the country.

He ran a chain of thirty-two hospitals in the United States, and twenty-three hospitals and nursing homes spread across Europe and Asia. He was well-acclaimed and had won numerous awards.

Dr Sanjay Sachdev understood that the manoeuvre made by his pilots to descend while attempting to circumnavigate the thunderstorm had gone in vain. They were flying over the Mogollon Rim in the American state of Arizona. The frequent lightning indicated dangerous consequences. The pilot used all his technical knowledge and skills to keep the aircraft going despite the engine failure. But the private plane began to get out of control.

The co-pilot came out of the cabin with a worried expression and requested the doctor to use a parachute and jump from the aircraft, while they tried to steer the plane to safety. He explained that the situation was precarious, and at any moment, they could lose control of the aircraft and crash. In fact, if they survived the perilous situation, it would be nothing less than a miracle.

Dr Sanjay was not a person to give up without a fight. He rejected the proposal of the co-pilot. Suddenly, the plane gave a big jolt, and the co-pilot, a steward and the air hostesses were thrown sideways, crashing against the windows of the jetliner. Not wasting any more time, the co-pilot, with great difficulty, opened the emergency exit door and urged the doctor, his employer, to jump before the plane crashed into one of the canyons. His safety belt had saved the doctor from any injury, but the jolt had badly shaken him up.

The jet was flying over the Salt River in Tonto National Forest with its deep canyon, bisecting the entire length of the wilderness. Looking at the panicky expressions of the crew members, the doctor realized the hopelessness of the situation. He saw all of them holding parachutes. It dawned upon him that they were only waiting for him. Once he jumped, they would follow suit. Dr Sanjay removed his safety belt and hurriedly wore his parachute, and without looking down, took a plunge in the sky. It was pitch black, with the dark clouds covering the moon and stars—only to be intermittently cut by the lightning that illuminated the sky every few minutes.

He descended towards the earth. Parachuting in a thunderstorm with high-velocity winds was extremely risky. He pulled the pin, and the parachute opened. But, as luck would have it, the slider failed to work, and the parachute inflated at a rapid speed, resulting in the damage of the fabric and suspension lines. The doctor started falling towards the earth fast. The partially-opened chute did curtail his descent from 120 miles-an-hour to almost half the speed, but it seemed that death was imminent. He braced himself for a hard landing. He let his fate take over.

In what seemed like his last moments, he closed his eyes and waited for the impact. However, luckily for him, he fell into the fast-flowing Salt River, entwined in the parachute. The force of the fall was so great that he hurt himself as he entered the water. Writhing in pain, he went deep down into the river. He struggled frantically and was somehow able to free himself of the parachute. Using all his strength, he reached the surface and swam towards one of the banks, partially against the current. He managed to swim to safety but was completely exhausted.

He had spent two years in the academy during his training as a military doctor, and that had prepared him to overcome such obstacles. He had learned to be a fighter and not to succumb until his last breath. He thanked his training days for helping him survive. Just then, lightning struck, and the weather condition worsened.

Dr Sanjay's plane was headed in the westward direction towards Phoenix where he was scheduled to attend a medical conference. He was not sure whether his ten-million-dollar jetliner or his crew had survived. He was not as worried about his plane as he was about the safety and survival of his crew members. In that weather, it seemed unlikely. But this was no time to ponder over their survival. He needed to save himself. He was in the Tonto National Forest, known to be infested with wild animals. He was all by himself, without any support or weapon. He tried to adjust his eyes to the darkness and look for any dwelling unit where he could seek shelter. But there was none in that wilderness.

He had no idea what lay in store for him, but he assumed that in case he moved towards the south, he would be able to reach the camp office of the national forest and then to the nearest city, Claypool. His destination was Phoenix, where two thousand doctors had gathered just to listen to the latest discoveries made by his advanced Research & Development (R&D) Centre in Boston for the cure of cancer. A major breakthrough had been made in the cure of the dreaded disease using a new technique.

He realized that he would have to think fast if he wanted to survive the forest. He remembered reading, a long time ago, that the US Highway 60 traverses a winding route through the canyon and descends close to the river at the bottom before moving towards the city of Claypool in the south. He also knew that Tonto National Forest is the fifth largest national forest in the United States and the largest of the six national forests in Arizona, inhabited by wild animals.

He moved south, through the thick and deep forest. The trail led to another rivulet, the sound of which brought the entire forest alive. He could not see any camp unit established by the authorities in that part of the woods. It was possibly not the season, he thought. He was thoroughly drenched and freezing from the cold.

Amidst the alarmed snorting of bears, he found himself peering through the dense vegetation of ponderosa pine, maple and oak trees. Moving through the myriad plants that surrounded him, he suddenly stumbled upon a colony of a harmful species of ants. The doctor was petrified to see thousands of those ants emerging from nowhere and beginning to climb up his shoes. He had probably stepped on an anthill and disturbed them, for they swarmed around him and began making their way up to his ankles. He knew that the bites of that large a number of ants could be highly injurious. He tried to shake them off, jumping around and stomping his shoes. But the moment his feet landed on the ground, more ants climbed up again. These ants were known to feed on carcasses; he just did not want to end up becoming their meal.

Just then, lightning struck a tree close to him, resulting in some branches catching fire. Before he was completely taken over by those creatures, he picked up a burning branch that had fallen close to him and waved it at the ants at his feet. They immediately stopped their assault and scattered away from him. With the help of the light of the fire, he was able to roll up his pants and brush off the ants on his legs. The swarm disappeared under the ground in no time, but before they could regroup, he ran from there, making sure to pick up another broken branch and light it using the first one. With burning torches in each hand, he could gain the upper hand on any animal that might attack. Dr Sanjay now moved towards the southern side of the river.

While moving cautiously, he suddenly wondered as to what a successful doctor and chairman of an extremely profitable organization was doing in this wilderness. He pressed his lips, cursing himself for agreeing to attend the medical conference in the first place. 'How could this happen to him?' he wondered.

Dr Sanjay was tall, well-built, physically strong and mentally tough even at the age of fifty-five. Being highly successful and a sought-after surgeon, he had become very proud of himself and developed a sense of superiority. But this situation was forcing him to think differently. A thought crept into his mind, 'How could poisonous ants or animals looking for a prey, at this hour of the night, in the deep forest where every life was in danger, possibly distinguish between a successful, rich human being and an unsuccessful one? For predators, the flesh was flesh and blood was blood. Their only motive was to satisfy their hunger. Just because he had saved thousands of lives during his illustrious career did not make him invincible. Could he bribe these predators with his knowledge, skill or money? The answer was a big NO. Could he bargain for his life in exchange for the medals received from the president of the United States for his services? Would it affect these animals if they were to know that this human being lost in the forest was the winner of several prestigious prizes in the field of medicine? The answer, again, was a big NO. He had to fend for himself.'

He started running south but stopped abruptly when he noticed some movement in the bushes ahead. He quickly realized that any further movement in the same direction could take him into the jaws of death. The torch in his hand was almost burnt out, and there was no time to light another. As he noticed a pair of shining eyes leering at him, the doctor threw down the torch he held and ran to a tree, climbing it. He was quick to clamber up and grab a branch firmly. But as he did so, he felt sharp teeth pulling his trousers down. He had no idea what animal was trying to pull him, but he could hear the growls. He held on to the branch using all his strength and worked hard to set his foot free from the dreadful animal's teeth digging into his trousers, tearing it apart. He instinctively lifted his other foot and slammed it on the nose of the beast with full force. It set him free and without looking down, he climbed up further to reach a safe distance from the blood-thirsty beast below. For a moment, the dark clouds parted and allowed moonlight to penetrate. He noticed that there were several wolves under the tree looking upwards, staring in his direction. Not sure of their intention, he decided to stay where he was.

It was 3.00 a.m. by his watch. The Rolex was undamaged even after being submerged in the Salt River. Another three hours would bring dawn. He decided to remain in the tree until the sun rose. It would keep him safe and also give him a clear view of his surroundings in daylight.

Some dark clouds dispersed with the breeze, and in the moonlight, he saw the wolves at the foot of the tree, waiting patiently for him. He did not close his eyes even for a second for the next three hours. Each passing minute seemed like an hour.

When the sun rose, Dr Sanjay's eyes were aching. He was thirsty and hungry. The wolves were nowhere to be seen, and he let out a sigh of relief. From where he sat, high on a branch, he was able to see the Salt River. He realized he had no alternative but to get back in the water. He would have to swim across to the other bank to be able to reach the southern campsite at the Tonto National Forest.

After having cautiously climbed down the tree, he started pacing towards the river ban. It was then, to his right at a distance, he saw a pair of cougars lying lazily on the bank, basking in the morning sun. The sight of these cougars—also known as panthers or mountain lions in the region—sent chills down Dr Sanjay's spine. The terrified surgeon did not want them to catch him before he reached the water. Slowly, he started steering left to create more distance between him and the panthers. When it seemed that he now had about a hundred yards between him and the panthers, he stopped and looked in their direction—they were still lying there, with no care for their surroundings. They were probably fast asleep, he thought. He decided it would be safe to go to the river, and once he was in the water, he would be able to swim away.

Dr Sanjay made out of the row of trees and bolted across the open patch of land before the river bank. As he ran, he looked over his shoulder to his right, praying the predators were not coming after him. But he was safe. He plunged into the cold water and began swiftly swimming away from the bank. After a few quick strokes, he put his head out of the water and turned to look back. He got the shock of his life. The cougars were jumping into the water and coming after him. He panicked. He had not realized that they could swim, and he had no idea how he was going to escape those dangerous and powerful creatures. If they caught him in the middle of the river, there was no chance that he would survive.

He was still much ahead of them. But they were gaining speed. He continued his swift strokes towards the other bank.

And as he turned to look back, he saw the beasts paddling away to the other side. Dr Sanjay raised his head to see a herd of deer that had come out of the forest to drink water. The cougars decided to go for the deer, leaving him in the river.

The doctor, seeing his way out, swam the final distance using all his strength. He rested on the other side, keeping an eye out for any kind of attack. His arms were searing with pain, so was the rest of his body. After resting for a while, he mustered enough strength and ran in the direction of the camp office at the border of the forest. Out of sheer fatigue, he blacked out just as he reached the camp.

James Gardner, the ever-vigilant forest officer—sipping coffee in his office—saw the doctor collapse. The officer called out for his assistant as he rushed towards the stranger. His assistant hurried out of the office with a medical kit in one hand and a shotgun in the other.

When Dr Sanjay regained consciousness, he found himself on a bed. With much difficulty, he lifted his arm to check the time on his watch. It was 2.00 p.m.! He had been unconscious for almost six hours. He was injured, but being alive mattered to him more. Just then, the forest officer walked into the room. The doctor wanted to express his gratitude to the officer but could only mumble a few inaudible words. He needed some more time to regain his strength.

The officer's assistant gave him some soup, and he drank it up. James recognized Dr Sanjay and readily agreed to aid him in whichever manner he could.

With James' help, Dr Sanjay tried to call his office in New York and then the organizers in Phoenix. But, as luck would have it, the thunderstorm had damaged the phone lines. He could not reach for help and seek support through telephone.

The forest officer offered to take him to a car-rental agency in Claypool where he could hire a vehicle and drive to Phoenix. Dr Sanjay, who had regained his strength by now, was eager to continue his journey. James saw to it that the doctor was administered painkillers, anti-tetanus injections and other first-aid medication, and then he drove him to Claypool.

At the agency, Dr Sanjay's first thought was to inform his family and his staff of his survival. He was equally worried about his crew. He made calls to his family and staff members and was informed that although his jetliner had crashed, his crew had survived. They were injured and were recuperating in a hospital at Phoenix. His family, in fact, had been in a state of shock and had left all hopes of his survival. The phone call was a big relief to his wife, Sonia and his daughters. They had been praying for his well-being from the moment they had come to know about the mishap.

'So the plane did crash,' Dr Sanjay froze at the thought. But he was much relieved about his crew and started feeling better. He was now keen to get to the conference at Phoenix by nightfall. James arranged for a chauffeur-driven car to take him to Phoenix. The doctor thanked him profusely for all his assistance. After an hour, he left for Phoenix.

On the way, as he sat in the latest model of the Chevy he had hired, a thought flashed across Dr Sanjay's mind that brought a smile to his face. It was only a few hours back, before boarding his private jetliner, that he had his favourite drink—two fingers of Johnnie Walker Blue Label whiskey—in his extravagant and comfortable palatial house in New York where he had attendants on his beck and call, serving him and taking care of his needs and desires. And what a contrast the last twenty-four hours had been…him fighting every minute for survival.

They had covered a distance of 65 km when the Chevy started to jerk in the middle of nowhere. His driver stopped the car to check the engine and see what was wrong. It stuttered incessantly. He could not understand the fault and tried to ignite the engine again. The car seemed to have broken down. Dr Sanjay stepped out. It was getting dark, and he was once again stranded. He looked in all directions for any sign of life or help. He noticed a small, dimly-lit hut about two hundred yards away from the national highway and decided to seek help from the occupants of the dwelling while the driver attended to the car.

He walked towards the house, hoping to call his manager and arrange for another car and knocked on the door. A frail woman, in her seventies, opened the door. She looked poor. He asked her if he could make a call. She told him that she did not have any such facility. However, she invited him into her tiny cottage. She lived in a single room, and there was barely any furniture in the house. The room contained a dilapidated bed and an old cooking range in a corner. The bedsheet was worn-out and the curtains, torn. The woman was extremely poor.

There was a six-year-old child lying on the bed. He seemed sick. It started to rain and the woman was quick to shut the window. She offered the doctor a loaf of bread, applying some homemade jam on it. The doctor took the loaf humbly and began to eat it.

He was amazed to see someone living this far away from the nearest town. She looked at his inquisitive and thoughtful expression, and understood what was going on in his mind. She explained her situation to him. Until the previous year, her husband, son and daughter-in-law had been with her. All of them were involved in cultivating farmlands near their cottage. They had a tractor-trolley on which they would load their agricultural goods for selling in the two nearby towns around 60 miles on either side.

The previous year, after selling their produce, they were travelling on the highway when they were hit and overrun by a speeding container. All three of them died on the spot when the container turned and fell on them. The old woman was the only one left to take care of her grandchild, who was unwell and bed-ridden due to a terminal disease. The city hospital doctors had told her it was brain cancer. The tumour had developed, and it hampered the movements of the six-year-old child. There was liquid in his brain that needed to be drained out by a surgical procedure.

Whatever little money she had was already used for the treatment of her sick grandchild. He was also suffering from leukaemia. Dr Sanjay knew everything about tumours and cancers, but he was tired and thought it improper to ask her any question in case he upset her. He, however, did compare his status, fame and wealth with that of the poor and unfortunate woman who lived in such poor conditions and fended for herself and the child.

The woman got up from her broken chair and said that it was time for her prayers. Kneeling down and turning her face, she asked the doctor if he wanted to pray to the Almighty God along with her. The agnostic doctor politely declined and told her that he was a non-believer and had neither offered prayers before nor would he bow down in front of any cross or statue made of wood or stone, in any place of worship. He arrogantly claimed to be an atheist, a complete believer of karma, meaning doing good deeds, rather than pleading before any statue. He had been to church only to attend weddings, he declared.

She turned her head towards a picture of Jesus Christ and a cross hanging on a wall, and prayed in silence for a short while. She was a firm believer in the power that prayers carried and never missed her evening ritual. It was her faith in God that kept her going. After her prayers were over, the doctor tried to instruct her on the theory of karma, and noticing her astonishment, he asked her justification for praying to God while living in such pitiable conditions. If God had answered her prayers, she would have been living a comfortable life. Her husband and children would be alive, and she would be as healthy as he was.

The woman told him that whenever she prayed, she asked for the recovery and well-being of her grandchild who was suffering. She also prayed to God to give her strength and the requisite funds to be able to admit the child to St George's Cancer Hospital in Boston. She explained to her bewildered guest that there was only one doctor, a well-renowned and one of the most famous doctors, Dr Sanjay, who could cure her grandchild of his dreaded disease. She said that she always prayed to God to create such circumstances that she would somehow meet that qualified surgeon who would then cure her only grandchild by skilfully performing an operation that only he could perform.

She also said that God had not answered her prayers till now, but she had full faith in Him. One day, he would fulfil her desire and give her the requisite strength and money so that she would be able to take her grandson to Dr Sanjay.

Stunned and speechless, Dr Sanjay stared at her in disbelief. Tears rolled down his cheeks. He stood transfixed for a moment. Then he sat down on the broken chair and thought to himself whether all that had happened was a coincidence or divine intervention. God was indeed great.

He recollected the sequence of events: there was a thunderstorm that caused a malfunction in his jetliner and made the flight dangerous. He jumped from the jet with a defective parachute but was saved because he fell into the Salt River. He experienced assaults by poisonous ants, wolves and cougars. Lightning had struck the tree and saved him. And then the car had broken down. All that had happened because a supernatural power had to answer the woman's prayers and make the doctor reach her small cottage, which would otherwise have been impossible. He was such a busy surgeon that anyone seeking an appointment with him had to wait for months.

He realized that things had not happened by chance. They were a spark of the divine. Dr Sanjay's arrogance disappeared. Nature had, time and again, given him chances to come out of the materialistic world and serve destitute and helpless people who had nothing to offer except prayers, but he, being an atheist, had never understood the signals so received by him. He had been a businessman all through his life.

Dr Sanjay Sachdev then, to the amazement of the poor woman, revealed his true identity. He examined the sick child and promised her to treat him without any cost. He also assured her that he would perform the operation as soon as possible.

He was overwhelmed with the purity with which the woman had bowed before the cross and prayed with utmost sincerity. Her prayers had been answered.

He realized that the world moved, existed and lived only through God's will and God's will alone. God had been with him all along, saving him from every danger. All those were no ordinary coincidences. The spark of the divine had triggered it all.

For the first time in his life, Dr Sanjay Sachdev went down

on his knees and prayed. He understood that he was a nobody in front of God. There and then he turned into being a believer, realizing the true strength of prayers.

A Lover's Message

This story revolves around a dejected, depressed lover, who for some reasons and under certain circumstances is unable to trace his beloved.

The idea to write this story was thought of way back in the 1990s by the late legendary actor Joy Mukherjee and his wife Neelam Mukherjee. The founder of Filmalaya, the Padma Shri Sasadhar Mukerjee (brother-in-law of Sh. Ashok and Sh. Kishore Kumar) wanted to make a film on this theme. Joy Mukherjee's son, Sujoy Mukherjee, has decided to make a film on the idea propounded by his father in the last decade. He, as such, had approached the authors to write the story and screenplay for a forthcoming film bearing the same title. The authors have taken up the assignment to write the screenplay and on completion thereof, the film will be released.

It was the spring of 1972. Major Raj Kiran Malhotra had recently returned to Delhi from the newly-formed nation of Bangladesh. He had fought valiantly against the Pakistani army and was awarded a medal for his bravery. Taking a ten-day leave of absence, he travelled to the picturesque state of Goa along with his course mate, Major Deewan. Lt V. K. Singh was deputed to receive them at Dabolim Airport and take them to the army guest house at Altinho in Panjim. But Major Raj preferred to stay in a private hotel near the Candolim Beach, so Lt Singh dropped them off at Casa Hotel. It was a beautiful afternoon with the outdoor temperature at 22°C. Dark clouds hovered in the sky, indicating the possibility of rain.

Once they had checked in at the hotel, both men went out to explore the nearby ruins of Fort Aguada, after which they planned to swim in the sea. Major Raj watched the waves as they lashed against the high walls of the fort, and he noticed a few girls swimming near the beach, just adjacent to it. The men went around the fort and stopped at the medium-sized canon facing the Arabian Sea. The date inscribed on it read 1502 AD, the year when the Portuguese had arrived in Goa. They stood on the fort looking out at the horizon and were fascinated by the beautiful scenery.

The men got into the water and began enjoying the sea waves. Major Raj wore dark goggles that added to the look of his handsome face and smart physique. He was tall, well-built and had crew-cut hair. As he waded further into the water, a strong wave struck him, throwing him off-balance. He fell backwards, and when he steadied himself, he found to his dismay that his expensive sunglasses had been swept away. Frantically, he looked for his Ray-Bans, but he could not find his *precious* goggles. They were precious because they were a gift from his father, who brought them from Singapore for his only son. As Major Raj looked for his goggles, he saw a girl walking towards the waves. She wore a similar pair of eyewear of the same brand. She was fair, had a perfect nose, large eyes and curly hair. She was very tall, her height almost matching up to the six-feet-two-inch-tall Major. She seemed to belong to a fairly rich and modern family, he thought.

Instinctively, he went towards the girl and told her to remove her goggles. He cautioned her not to wear them since he had just lost his pair to a wave. She could lose hers too. The girl smiled and removing the glasses said, 'Thank you, Sir. I shall be careful not to lose them.'

And then, she joined her friends.

Major Raj, a little dejected at losing his sunglasses, sauntered back to his hotel. The picture of the girl he had just met came to his mind. 'She was a hell of an attractive girl,' he spoke to himself. 'She could match any Hollywood actress.' After about an hour, as he sat beside the swimming pool in his hotel having a chilled beer, the same girl walked up to him.

'Are these your Ray-Bans?' She held up the pair for him to see.

'Oh, yes, yes! They are mine!' He got up with excitement. 'How come you have them? They were swept away, ma'am.'

She replied with a grin, 'Isn't it strange? About half-an-hour after you left, a wave came in and these glasses hit my left calf. I was barely able to catch them before the wave receded. You are lucky because you had told me about them; otherwise, I may not have been alert and on the lookout.'

Major Raj thanked her profusely and asked her to join him for a drink. They began to talk. He asked if she was staying at the same hotel. She told him she was a local inhabitant staying with her parents at Reis Magos, close to the Three Kings Church and Reis Magos Fort. Her name was Sara D'Souza, and she was pursuing her MBBS from Goa Medical College in Bambolim. She would become a doctor in a year's time and was keen on starting her internship in Bombay.

'Oh!' he said, 'You're a Christian. I am Raj Kiran Malhotra, a Punjabi from New Delhi. I'm a Major in the Corps of

Signals stationed at the Headquarters in Kolkata, in the Eastern Command.'

She understood what Eastern Command meant and nodded her head. She told him that she could make out from his looks that he was from the army. Two of her uncles had served in the defence services too. One had been an ace pilot, Squadron Leader Braganza, who had died in the 1965 war with Pakistan. The other, Lt Col James Braganza, was killed a few months ago in Dhaka while fighting the enemy. It was the Major's turn to show surprise. He had been directly appointed under Lt Col Braganza. He and his fellow officers referred to the senior as 'Goan Braggy', who was known for being an ace shooter and a daredevil.

'You are Goan Braggy's niece? I mean, Col Braganza? It's surely a small world,' he said and then continued in a sober tone. 'He fought valiantly alongside the Mukti Bahini in the Bangladesh war. I cannot believe that you are his niece. He died in the battlefield just a few yards from me.' The Major narrated the incident as though he were reliving it. 'Unfortunately, Lt Col Braganza was not there to witness the surrender of the Pakistani army,' he said, sadly.

Sara invited the Major to her house. She told him that her mother would be pleased to spend time with someone from the army, especially someone who had served under her brother and was with him in his last moments. Major Raj promised to pay a visit to her home and meet her mother. That night, the Major could hardly sleep. He was mesmerized by the beautiful, innocent and soft-spoken Sara D'Souza. He dreamt of her in his arms and both of them dancing in the banquet hall of his mess.

Next day Major Raj, along with Major Deewan, reached Villa Elvira, Sara's home, and met her parents. Throughout the talk, he kept glancing at Sara. She was not very receptive to his looks but understood that he was attracted to her. When the officers took leave of the family, he asked Sara if she could show him around as this was his first visit to the state.

Major Raj spent the next few days of his holiday with Sara and explored Goa. They visited the beaches, restaurants and churches. He was so attracted to her that at the end of his stay in Goa, he found it very difficult to leave Sara. His course mate pulled his leg at every chance, calling him a complete 'lost case', saying he was no good for the army anymore. Major Raj laughed it off and said it was just a crush that he had on the good-looking girl; he would soon get over it. But destiny had something else in store for him.

Months passed after which a vacancy came up in the Signals Corps at Altinho Hill in Goa. Major Raj opted for the posting as it was in Panjim, close to Reis Magos. He telephoned Sara and informed her of his moving to Goa. She understood the reason for his excitement. Soon, the Major was settled at the army accommodation at Altinho.

The next year was like living a dream for him. And after a year of courtship, Sara found herself totally in love with him too. Both spent as much time as they could with each other.

When Sara completed her MBBS, Major Raj called his parents and asked them to approach Sara's parents for the marriage alliance. His father, who was a Brigadier in the 1971 war, was now a Major general in the Eastern Command.

The senior Malhotras travelled to Goa to offer their proposal. They met Sara's parents but were in for a surprise when Sara's mother expressed her unwillingness to the alliance. She was against her daughter marrying an army officer, she said. Major Raj was at a loss. And his parents looked at him, confused.

When they asked for her reasons, she said that her family had already lost close relatives in wars. She did not want another loss in her family. Both her brothers had died so young, they were only in their thirties.

General Malhotra tried his best to convince the D'Souza family, but the mother would not budge from her decision. Finally, Sara intervened and discussed the matter with her parents. She stubbornly insisted on marrying the Major. Her mother had to agree, but Mrs D'Souza placed her condition—that the ceremony would take place as per Christian customs in The Kings Church in Goa. Major Raj readily agreed. The wedding was set for a date four months later. Major Raj and Sara could not have been happier.

Two months before the wedding, Major Raj was transferred to Siachen Glacier located in the Himalayas, also known as the world's highest battlefield at the height of 21,000 feet. It is the area where the Line of Control (LOC) between India and Pakistan stands. The low temperatures—between -25 °C and -35 °C—could even dip to -50 °C. Army personnel had to first go through training so they could survive the cold.

Major Raj bid farewell to Sara and her family, and promised to return well in time for the wedding so that he could help with the preparations.

While at Siachen, he missed Sara a lot and wished he could just fly back to her. He longed for her and dreamt of spending their life together.

One night, as the officers slept in their tents, an avalanche hit their camp. The soldiers were caught off-guard and tried to save themselves, but it was too late. Twenty soldiers went missing. It was inferred that they had got buried deep in the snow, which meant a zero per cent chance of survival.

Rescue teams from Leh and Udhampur reached the site the next day. They dug through the 30-feet-deep snow with extreme difficulty. Eighteen of the missing soldiers were extricated, but they were only bodies. Two were still missing—Major Deewan and Major Raj Kiran. The news was flashed on TV and radio, and it reached the family in Goa.

Sara was shocked and shattered on hearing about the disaster. She could not believe what had happened. She wept bitterly and prayed that her Raj, somehow, had survived. His body had not been found as yet, so she hoped against hope that he was still alive. She started going to church every morning to light a candle and pray for the well-being of her beloved.

After a week of digging and searching the area, the rescue teams found the body of Major Deewan. They continued to look for Major Raj but ultimately, losing all hope, they declared him dead. After hearing this news, Sara was inconsolable. This was what her parents had feared, and it was the reason they did not want their daughter to marry an army officer.

Sara's father came to a decision. He believed that getting her married to a Christian businessman would be the right thing to do, and that a new relationship would heal her wounds. Sara was against her father's wish, but she did not have the strength to argue with him. She gave in and married George, the son of her father's oldest friend.

It had been days; he didn't know how many. Major Raj was alive. He had been thrown down a deep ravine. And it was only because of his dear Sara that he had survived. His thoughts about her had given him the strength to endure the bitter cold and terrible conditions. He found stocks of an earlier camp buried in the snow and so survived on canned cheese and dry fruits. After almost a month of the avalanche, a patrolling troop found him lying in a cave, unconscious. He was immediately taken to the army hospital. It took him two months to recuperate. Only after that, he was in a position to go to Goa.

Meanwhile, his parents were informed that he had survived. His father spoke to Mr D'Souza, giving him the incredible news, but he told him it would take a few weeks for his son to fully recover. Mr D'Souza, no doubt, was very happy. But he was in a dilemma. Sara's wedding was around the corner. Preparations had been made. And Sara was finally ready. He decided against giving his daughter the news. Once the wedding ceremony had taken place, there would be no turning back.

Major Raj went straight to Sara's house from the airport. Mr D'Souza welcomed him, made him sit down and offered him a drink. The two spoke for some time, and Major Raj described how he was rescued. He also told Mr D'Souza that it was Sara's love that had actually kept him alive.

Mr D'Souza now broke the news about Sara's wedding to a Goan. He told the Major that she was indeed in love with him, but that the news of his demise had changed everything. By the time news of the Major's survival had reached them, it was too late. Sara was on the threshold of a new life, and her parents had thought it better not to stop her from going for it. He told the Major that he was sorry for what happened, but maybe it was according to God's will. He also requested him not to reveal the truth to Sara. It would only create problems in her married life. It was best not to let her know he was alive. She had moved on and married, and was now living a happy life with her husband.

Major Raj was devastated. He could not believe or accept the harsh reality of his fate. He remained in Goa and took to drinking alcohol. His father came to Goa and took him back to Delhi. After a couple of months of stay at home with his parents, the Major opted for a posting in Kupwara near the LOC area. Kupwara was a small district in the beautiful Kashmir Valley, but it was the area most attacked near the border. It was rumoured that infiltrators entered India through that part of the country. Major Raj Kiran was a daredevil, but more than that he did not care anymore. He could not get Sara out of his mind. She was too deep in it.

His father sent him several offers of marriage that came for him, but Major Raj could not even think of any other girl. It was impossible for him. Time passed, but he never married. His father retired from the army and moved from Delhi to Wellington in Tamil Nadu where he had bought a villa. He began to live there peacefully, as did Field Marshal Sam Manekshaw. Both were good friends and played golf together at the Wellington Club. Years passed by, and Major Raj lived a secluded life.

Raj Kiran was promoted to the rank of Colonel and posted to a small island, the last point of land owned by India in the south, close to Sri Lanka. The Indian tricolour flag was flown there to mark the last point of territory under Indian occupation. It was an island where for miles there was no other land in sight, but for two small naval and army base camps established by the Indian authorities. During his stay on the island, Col Raj was always reminded of Sara because it was here that the Indian Ocean merged with the Arabian Sea, and the mention of the sea sparked memories of his Sara and their days together in Goa.

Once, it was midnight when he sat on a shore of the island with a bottle of wine in his hand. He blamed his fate for his failed love life. His colleague, Col S.C. Roy, sat beside him. The latter knew about his love for Sara. He gave Col Raj an idea. 'If you really love her, why don't you send her a message?'

A Lover's Message

'I have vowed never to meet her, my friend, and I won't break my vow,' Col Raj replied.

'But you can send her a message in a wine bottle? If you truly love her, it will reach her. Just write to her and throw the bottle there,' Col Roy said, pointing in the direction of the water. 'Do you really love Sara?'

'Of course, I do.' Saying so, Col Raj took a piece of paper and wrote a letter addressed to his beloved:

3 May 1997

Dearest of all Sara,

I sincerely hope that you are living a happy married life in your beautiful home in Goa. You would be taking good care of your husband and children.

I am writing to you to see whether there is a God. If there is one, then I am sure this letter—through which I want to inform you that I am still alive and in love with you—will eventually reach you. If there is no such thing as a divine power, then like our love story, this letter will also reach the bottom of the Arabian Sea and remain there.

Sara, I have vowed to never get married to anyone else. I live the life of a bachelor. I am now fifty-two and have reached the rank of Colonel in the army. It has now been more than twenty-five years since I met you in 1972, but I remember each, and every day spent with you in Goa. I wanted to tell you that I will remember you as long as I live.

I will be retiring in six years from now, and I intend to spend my life thereafter in my father's villa in Wellington in Tamil Nadu.

I do remember our first meeting at Candolim Beach and

how you returned my goggles at the Casa Hotel. I will never forget the time I spent with you.

At present, I am based on an island near Sri Lanka.

If at all, this letter reaches you, then it will re-establish my faith in God.

Yours and yours forever,
Raj Kiran Malhotra

He folded the letter, emptied the wine bottle, and after inserting the letter in it, corked it securely. Walking to the edge of the water, he made sure to throw the bottle as far into the sea as possible, so that it would be carried away by the waves. He turned and smiled at his colleague.

Col Raj continued with his duties as a devoted officer serving his country. In the days to come, he forgot about the bottle and his heartfelt message that it carried.

∽

Vineet Sharma belonged to a middle-class family in Jaipur. His father, Prem Kumar Sharma, was in government service and a contented man. But Vineet wanted to become rich overnight. He was an overly ambitious man. So, against his father's advice, he started trading in silver.

Vineet's business began to expand, and he invited his brother-in-law, Ramesh Singhvi, to work with him. Ramesh was as ambitious as Vineet, but he was unscrupulous too. Vineet committed the error of placing too much trust in his family member who had married his sister just a couple of months ago.

Ramesh opened fake bank accounts in the name of several clients by using phoney signatures. He manipulated books, showing deposits against the payment of the purchase of silver on behalf of clients, whereas instead of paying the investors, the money was transferred to his fake accounts. He later withdrew cash from those bogus accounts to pay off his debts incurred in horse racing and speculative share transactions, without the knowledge of his brother-in-law.

In five years, Ramesh embezzled almost seven crore rupees through this hidden manipulation. And when the auditors and investors eventually caught the fraud, it was too late. When it was brought to the knowledge of Vineet, he was furious, and he lodged a complaint with the police. But before the police could apprehend Ramesh, he absconded to an unknown destination.

Vineet's world came crashing down. He could not bear such a huge deficit and loss in business. He was liable to pay to his investors nevertheless. He sold his house and office space in Jaipur, and that fetched him four crore rupees. He also encashed all his fixed deposits, but it was not enough to compensate the full amount that was stolen by Ramesh.

Meanwhile, the police sent several search parties looking for the absconding culprit. They were about to arrest Ramesh from a hideout in Bhiwani in Haryana, but he drank rat poison and ended his life. It was a difficult time for Vineet. He had a long list of clients who were still to be paid in lieu of the money pilfered by his brother-in-law, and his family had to come to terms with Ramesh's cheating, and then Vineet's sister becoming a widow.

Vineet went to Goa. He had once bought a property at Candolim. The sale of that apartment at Sea View Estate could fetch him at least fifty lakh rupees and help him settle some of the investors.

Vineet's frustration began to grow when he was unable to sell his Goa property. His investors called him every day. He could not go back to Jaipur and face them, so he stayed on in Goa. All attempts at raising money were unsuccessful. Vineet took to drinking. One evening, in a drunken state, depressed as he was, he decided to end his life. He walked into the sea to bring an end to all his problems. But when a high wave took him further into the waters, a realization dawned on him—he desperately tried to save himself, gasping for breath. He clutched at an object, trying to keep himself afloat, but began to choke as water entered his lungs. He went into the water and then was thrown back up by undercurrents. As he came to the surface, a lifeguard in a rescue boat saw him and dived into the sea to save him from drowning. An unconscious Vineet was taken to a rehabilitation centre run by a Mrs Gonsalves, where he was revived by doctors.

Mrs Gonsalves was in her fifties, and she owned the centre that was situated near the Calangute Beach. She was a widow, and some six years ago, her only son had, in a drunken state, been swept away to death by the killer waves of the sea. Since then, she had taken it upon herself to try and save such people who, because of their inebriated state, were caught in the waves and faced death.

After a day's rest, Vineet thanked the lady and was about to leave the rehab centre when he was handed over a wine bottle. It was found clutched in his hand when he was saved by the lifeguard. Seeing a piece of paper inside the bottle, the guard and the others at the centre thought it could be of some meaning to Vineet, so they decided to give it back to him.

Instead of returning to his apartment, Vineet went to Casa Hotel to have his lunch. He uncorked the bottle, and on finding a letter in it written by a Col Raj Kiran six years ago, he was intrigued. He read the contents of the letter and realized that he was sitting in the same Casa Hotel, where the couple mentioned in the letter had met each other the first time.

Vineet read and re-read the letter. It was a message by a lover to his beloved of being alive and expressing his love for her. He wondered whether he had been saved by God to play a role in the lives of the two lovers. Maybe it was God's will that he must unite the couple, and that was why he had been given a second chance at life?

He could not trace Sara, but surely, he could go to Wellington. The letter was dated 3 May 1997, the Colonel named Raj Kiran Malhotra would have just retired, if at all he was alive. Vineet was astonished that the letter was intact even after six long years of being in the sea. He had a lot of issues of his own to resolve, but the thought of uniting the lovers brought a renewed purpose to his life.

He took a train to Coimbatore and from there took a taxi to Wellington Gymkhana Club. He enquired about Col Raj Kiran Malhotra and was informed that the Colonel had retired as a Brigadier and could be found on the golf course of the club.

Brig Raj Kiran recognized the bottle in the stranger's hand immediately. He took Vineet to Gunpowder Room at the club where they made themselves comfortable, and then they began their talk. The Brigadier told Vineet that he had always had an intuition that the wine bottle with the message in it would resurface one day. He also had the firm belief that when it resurfaced, it would straightaway reach the hands of his beloved, as had happened with his goggles.

He told Vineet about how his relationship with Sara had started. It was one of the strangest things to happen. He had cautioned only one girl out of all those who were in the water, and only she had found his Ray-Bans. That extraordinary meeting had later taken the shape of a relationship, and the time he spent with Sara was the best in his life. Brig Raj took Vineet to his home. The latter spent three days with him sharing his own experiences of losing every penny due to the fraud committed by his brother-in-law.

Brig Raj told Vineet that he had started believing in God after the manner in which the bottle had found its way into Vineet's hands. 'I have a firm belief that there is some past-life connection between you and me; otherwise, this bottle, thrown so many years back, wouldn't have been found by you in Goa of all the places, and of all the places, you wouldn't have read it at Casa Hotel. Somewhere in Goa, Sara lives with her husband. In case you can trace her whereabouts, I will be eternally grateful.'

Vineet promised Brig Raj that he would definitely help him find his Sara. When Vineet left for Goa, he carried the wine bottle and letter along with him.

During the journey, while he was deep in his thoughts, Vineet suddenly remembered what the Brigadier had said to him. 'That he had had a firm belief that one day, when the bottle resurfaced, it would straightaway reach the hands of his beloved, as had happened with his goggles.'

Vineet did not even know the full name of the owner of the rehab centre—the lady whose staff had saved him from death. But he remembered that she was a doctor. 'Could she be Sara?' He thought to himself.

He straightaway went to the rehab centre. The lady, Dr Gonsalves, was attending to a patient. Her attendant asked him to wait in the sitting room of the portion of the Portuguese cottage where she lived. The other rooms were used for treatment purposes.

He was impatiently waiting for her when his eyes fell on

her crockery cupboard. Neatly placed on a shelf, lay a pair of Ray-Ban sunglasses. As the lady doctor entered, he hastily asked her who the owner of the glasses was. The goggles seemed old but were placed carefully on the shelf as though they were a prized possession.

Mrs Gonsalves was surprised at the strange question. She told him it was something personal that she could not share with him. Vineet smiled and said that it was her staff who had handed the wine bottle to him a week back.

'Vineet, what has that bottle got to do with me?' she asked, perplexed.

Vineet replied, 'Ma'am, once you open the bottle and read what is inside it, you will certainly reveal the name of the owner of the sunglasses to me. Ma'am, please read it. It is a message from a lover to someone called "Sara",' he put emphasis on her name. 'The bottle was left in the sea near Sri Lanka, six years back, with a message, and it has reached you. Please read the message,' he politely requested her.

Mrs Gonsalves was astonished at his mention of her name. She slowly and with hands shaking, opened the cork and read the contents of the letter. Tears trickled down her eyes. She turned and looked at Vineet and asked him if he was a relative of Major Raj Kiran. Sara Gonsalves had loved the Major, but he had died in an avalanche at Siachen Glacier. She looked at him and said, her voice shaking, 'But if he died in 1973, how could he write a letter in 1997?'

'He is very much alive, ma'am, and waiting for you.'

Vineet told her that Major Raj Kiran was now Brigadier Raj Kiran Malhotra and that he retired from service and lived in Wellington.

He told her that the Brigadier had always believed in his

heart that the bottle thrown hundreds of miles away would one day reach her. While she kept on holding the letter, he picked up the telephone lying on a table and dialled the Brigadier's number. Vineet, without wasting any time, gave him the terrific news of having traced Sara. Then he handed the receiver to Sara.

Both could not speak for a few moments, as words gave way to pent-up emotions. Tears rolled down Sara's cheeks. They were tears of happiness. She was on cloud nine. Vineet left her alone to speak to her beloved, who had sacrificed his love and life for her sake.

Vineet came back to the sitting room after half an hour to find Sara still holding the phone and speaking to her Raj. He understood that both of them had a lot to say to each other; they were talking after a gap of thirty long years.

Sara and Raj were married the next Sunday. Many friends and relatives joined the ceremony at the Three Kings Church at Reis Magos. Fifty-four-year-old Sara, looking extremely beautiful in a white gown, walked down the aisle with her father escorting her. Next to the Father of the church, stood her prince charming, Brigadier Raj Kiran Malhotra, with a wedding ring, waiting for his bride. It seemed the years had not changed him at all. At fifty-eight, he stood tall and handsome just as he did on Fort Aguada in 1972. Vineet, his best man, stood beside him. The couple was proclaimed man and wife and, finally, the long wait was over.

During the outdoor luncheon party after the ceremony, the couple wore their respective Ray-Bans as was scheduled to happen thirty years ago.

A message carried in a wine bottle across the Arabian Sea, finally united a man with his beloved—his long lost love.

One month after the wedding, the happy couple, Sara and Raj, arrived in Jaipur. They convinced Vineet and his family to accept financial help from them that would clear the family's debts.

Acknowledgements

We would like to thank our parents, Shanker Kapoor and Rajni Kapoor, who have always been an inspiration. We would also like to extend our gratitude to our respective spouses, Punam Kapoor and Manisha Kapoor, for their unconditional support and valuable suggestions.

We also thank Anoo Chhathrath Nayyar, a friend and a journalist, for her vital suggestions, which has helped in breathing life into the characters we have created, and spending time in developing these stories, taking them to a much higher pedestal.

Aman, Mahima and Sagarika (chartered accountants and advocates), who handled the professional work, which allowed us to spend some time to re-visit places described in these stories. Paarth, Anachal and Ishaan, having studied abroad, provided insights about foreign locales.

We would also like to thank Surabhi Joneja, for her assistance in the editing and proofreading this book.

Last but not the least, we are thankful to the team of Rupa Publications for agreeing to promote this book under their aegis and publishing it.